# MURDER AT THE RACES

CARMEN RADTKE

MURDER AT THE RACES

By Carmen Radtke

*ISBN 978-1-9162410-3-9*

ALSO BY CARMEN RADTKE

False Play at the Christmas Party (a Jack Sullivan mystery)

A Matter of Love and Death (a Jack and Frances mystery)

The Case of the Missing Bride (an Alyssa Chalmers mystery)

Glittering Death (an Alyssa Chalmers mystery)

Walking in the Shadow

*This book is dedicated to the people of Adelaide, to horse lovers, and to everyone who - like me - spent unforgettable hours at the races.*
*I've taken a few liberties with Morphettville. The racecourse is and always has been one of the most exciting but also peaceful places to visit. Any shenanigans described in this novel only happened in my imagination. The beauty and wonder of the Morphettville racecourse is real, though.*

# MURDER AT THE RACES

Cast of Characters

At the Top Note:
Jack Sullivan, veteran and charming owner of the
Top Note
Bluey Fitzpatrick, his second-in-command
Marie Fitzpatrick, Bluey's resourceful wife
Dolores Barden, singer and star of the Top Note
Pauline Meara, Dolores' dresser and Frances's best friend
Tony Dixon, Pauline's fiancé and handy-man working
for Jack

Other characters:

Frances Palmer, Jack's girlfriend
Uncle Sal, aka Salvatore the Magnificent, Frances's
honorary uncle, ex-Vaudevillian

Robert Theodore Palmer, Frances's brother, a racecourse vet

Brocky, a racecourse blacksmith with a too good memory for hooves

Mr Dunne, manager of Morphettville racecourse

Mr Lucca, his assistant

Mr Henry, racecourse accountant

Dr O'Leary, racecourse doctor

Dr Gant, former racecourse vet

Andie Miller, a friend of Marie Fitzpatrick's

Sergeant Miller, her policeman husband

Arthur Dowling, a veteran and part of Jack's network

Kev and Paula Johnson, guesthouse owners and part of Jack's network

Assorted bookies, musicians and staff

# CHAPTER ONE

*T*he knife whirred past its target with less than an inch to spare, burying itself deeply into the wood. Frances expelled her held breath in a loud whoosh, but Uncle Sal shook his head in dismay. 'It's no good, love,' he said. 'Did you see how I went off my aim when I stepped back?"

She hadn't but then he was the professional, and she wasn't. She said, 'That's only to be expected. You haven't practiced in over two years.'

'It's not that. It's my gammy ankle, Frances. I can't risk it, not with you as target.' He flung the two remaining knives at the silhouette they'd painted onto a door that stood propped up centre-stage. They rose in an arc, making a full turn in the air, before embedding themselves blade-point between the outlined arms and chest.

'I don't mind,' she said. 'I trust you. And maybe we could put saw-dust on the stage, to make it less slippery.' She slid a sequinned shoe over the ground. The floorboards weren't too smooth, if she were honest, because they were usually covered by black felt, but that had been taken off for their rehearsal. The room looked naked, its night-time glamour replaced by a workmanlike atmosphere for a few hours before the magic got switched back on. Cinderella, waiting for pumpkin-time. Frances wondered if Uncle Sal felt the same about his surroundings. Probably not, for an old vaudeville artist a stage was a stage, wherever he was.

He said, 'Thanks, love, but it's no use, even if Dolores and the band wouldn't mind looking like they're playing in a barn. We'll just have to spruce up our juggling act a bit, that's all.' He shrugged off his disappointment with his usual grace, but she could see that it hurt.

'Are you sure?' she said.

'Oh yes. Can you imagine what your mother would have to say if I so much as hurt a hair on your head? I'm not even thinking of what Jack would do.'

'Or I, in that case,' a voice said behind her back.

'Rob!' Her big brother dropped his suitcase as she jumped into his arms. 'What are you doing here?'

'Checking up on you, of course. What do you expect when I find out that my little sister has taken up with a night club owner, Mum's lodger has been seduced by a singer and Uncle Sal is returning to the stage, all within the span of a few months?' He held her at arm's length. 'I wouldn't have recognised you on the street, that's for sure. Since when are you a platinum blonde? No wonder you set tongues buzzing.'

'Don't be silly,' she said, whipping off the wig. 'Uncle Sal will tell you all there is to know while I get changed.'

She smiled to herself as she ran towards the dressing room at the back of the stage. Things surely couldn't get much better than this, she thought, as she took off the sequinned and tasselled dress Miss Francesca wore, to become plain old Frances Palmer again. Despite today's setback, Uncle Sal looked ten years younger since they'd started rehearsing for their part in the charity show that Jack was going to stage in the Top Note, Adelaide's safest and, for her, best night club. Having Rob turn up on their doorstep made her joy complete. She'd wanted him for months to meet Jack and Dolores and all the rest but coming all the way from Queensland when everyone was penny-pinching would have been impossible.

The men waited for her in the passage. Rob gave her an appraising look. 'You've grown up to be quite a looker since I last saw you,' he said with brotherly insouciance. 'I bet Uncle Sal has his hands full keeping you out of trouble, from what he told me.'

Heat rose in her cheeks. She gave Uncle Sal a questioning glance. He'd promised to keep quiet about her and Jack Sullivan's part in a murder investigation earlier this year. He shook his head imperceptibly.

Rob chuckled. 'I can't wait to lay eyes on this paragon of yours, who's charmed my little sister and Mum at the same time. Uncle Sal tells me he is the whitest of men, but that I'll have to see for myself.' He grinned. 'I am the head of the family after all.'

She gave him a fond box on the shoulder, wishing he'd hush his voice a bit, as a door opened and Jack stepped out of the room. He stretched out his hand and said, 'I couldn't help but overhear that somewhat effusive praise. I hope you're not too disappointed.' His sleepy eyes held a decided twinkle.

'Not at all.' Rob shook Jack's hand, faint colour rising in his pale skin. It made him look younger, more like an overgrown schoolboy than a fully qualified vet and father of one. Frances had to refrain from smoothing down his unruly hair.

Jack said, 'In that case, maybe you'd care to join us tonight for dinner, unless you've got other plans?'

'I promised Mum I'd spend the evening with her. Maybe afterwards?'

'Fine.' Jack stroked Frances's cheek with his thumb. 'How did the rehearsal go?'

Uncle Sal turned away from them as she said, 'Why don't you watch us the next time?'

'If I can. I've got a ton of paperwork waiting for me. See you later, kiddo, Uncle Sal. Nice to meet you, Rob.'

'Bye.' Frances gave him a quick kiss on the cheek, before she slipped her arm through her brother's. 'Now, out with it, Rob. What brings you here? And where's Lucy and Junior?'

He swung his suitcase in his free hand. 'No need to worry, I'm here for a job.'

'A job? But you've got one, haven't you?' Her heartbeat quickened.

'Sure do. It's only, well, most farmers can't pay their bills, Frances, and some of them haven't been able to make a single payment since the end of 1930, so I've got a bit of time off the practice.'

She heard Uncle Sal whistle under his breath as she took in the implications.

Rob put his suitcase down to pat her hand. 'It's fine, Frances. Honestly.'

They left the club through the back door. She blinked as the sunshine hit her. Not even noon, and already the heat settled in over the city.

'Miss Frances?' Bluey hailed her as he followed them. 'If you'll give me two minutes, I'll get the Ford.'

'Thank you,' she said. 'Bluey, this is my brother, Rob. Rob, I want you to meet Bluey. He's Jack right-hand man and a good friend.'

The men shook hands, in that slow way they employed when trying to take someone else's measure. Frances smiled to herself. Rob hadn't acted like that with Jack, but then she couldn't imagine anyone doing that. Jack had the same air of easy command that Uncle Sal exuded on stage.

Rob gave her a brotherly poke with his elbow as soon as Bluey was out of earshot. 'I'm impressed with you folks. How the other half lives, eh?'

'They work just as hard as you do,' Uncle Sal said. 'Probably harder, especially Jack.'

'I didn't mean to criticise, Uncle Sal. Surely you know that.'

Bluey drove up and pulled the car into the curb. Without asking, he stowed Rob's suitcase away. 'Where to?' he asked as Uncle Sal climbed onto the passenger seat. Rob and Frances sat in the back. 'Your home?'

'Yes,' said Frances, surprised at the question.

Rob cleared his throat. 'If you don't mind, I need to go down to the racecourse first and drop off my luggage, if it's not too much to ask.'

'Which one? Morphettville or Victoria Park?

'Morphettville.'

'Sweet.' Bluey started the motor.

'But aren't you staying with us?' Frances asked.

'Where? You've got no room unless I kip on the sofa, Frances, and anyway my new job comes with digs.'

'What is it you're going to do?' asked Uncle Sal.

'Working as a travelling vet for the racecourses.' Rob's eyes shone. He'd always loved high-bred horses, Frances recalled, but most of his working life involved sheep, cattle and workhorses.

'What about Lucy and your son?'

He ruffled his light-brown hair that was the same colour as hers until it stood up in spikes. 'They're fine back home. It's only for a few months, and then I'll return to my old job. I really need the money, Frances, and this was too good to miss.'

She leant against his shoulder. 'I'm not complaining. It's bonzer to have you back for a bit.'

At the racecourse, Rob was gone for less than five minutes, to drop off his luggage and get his key.

'Maggie will be chuffed to bits,' Uncle Sal said while they were waiting outside the gates. 'She doesn't say anything, but she misses that boy, and her grandson.' He paused. 'I only hope it won't spoil her visit to Melbourne, knowing that Rob's here.'

'I jolly well hope not. She's been looking forward to seeing Uncle Fred and Aunt Millie for ages. And we've saved so hard for the train fare.' Frances's wages as a switchboard operator covered the mortgage and everyday bills, but they'd been pressed to save a penny until they'd taken in a lodger just before Easter. 'And she'll only been gone for a month.'

Rob strolled towards them, his empty hands dangling. He still looked like a gangly youth, Frances thought, despite his twenty-seven years.

'Thanks,' he said to Bluey as he got back in. 'I appreciate that.'

Bluey nodded. It took a while for him to loosen up around new people. As vexing as it could be, it made him invaluable when it came to dealing with unwanted people in the club. They all underestimated the quiet, burly man with the blank face. Frances hoped he and

Rob would become friends. She wanted everyone she cared about to love her brother.

'How did you know where to find us?' Uncle Sal asked. 'Don't tell me Maggie let you run off as soon as you'd set foot in the house.'

'She was gone, covering from someone at the soup kitchen,' Rob said. 'Miss Edna told me to try my luck at the Top Note and give your name as the magic word. It sure worked.'

Frances's cheeks grew warm again. It seemed as if the whole neighbourhood took her relationship to Jack for granted. Or Uncle Sal's. Or their lodger Phil's involvement with Dolores Bardon, the ravishing singer whose husband had died a few weeks before the war ended in 1918. Alright, she admitted to herself, there were a few reasons why the Palmer household could be linked with the Top Note in the minds of people.

It wasn't that she was ashamed of it, on the contrary, but she was so happy in the present that she didn't want to think about the future. Or maybe deep down she wondered if she and Jack had a future together. He might get bored with her.

She suppressed that thought as soon as it had popped up in her head. Whatever the future held, it would be for a good reason. For now, it was enough to have Jack, and to prepare for her stage debut with Uncle Sal, and enjoy Rob's company. Plenty to be thankful for.

Bluey parked in his accustomed spot. 'Thanks,' she said as they alighted.

'You're welcome as usual,' he said, giving her a smile that lit his whole face. 'See you tomorrow.'

They stepped into the passage. A light breeze stirred the air, sending tiny dust and sand particles floating. No matter how much time Mum spent cleaning, the Australian wind always managed to find a way to invade houses, bringing sand in its wake. Nobody wanted to seal windows and doors anyway. You needed the wind to beat back the heat that settled like a blanket in closed rooms.

Rob followed her to the back door. Mum sat on the porch, shelling peas into a bowl on her lap.

He tiptoed over to her on silent feet. 'I'm home,' he said, touching her sleeve.

Mum looked up with a startled expression. 'Rob!' She hugged him with a fierce intensity that surprised Frances.

'Hold it,' said, Rob, rescuing the bowl from falling over.

'Oh Rob. I've missed you so much.'

Uncle Sal who stood behind Frances, took her hand. 'Let's give them some space,' he said into her ear.

She followed him inside, still unsettled by the passion in Mum's voice. She'd thought that Mum was content with her life but obviously she, Uncle Sal, their friends and neighbours weren't enough. Mum must have been unhappy many times, being unable to visit her son and his family because of the money worries that dogged everyone's life since 1929, but she'd never said a word. Or maybe Frances hadn't listened, because she was too caught up in her own world. Well, now Mum had Rob back, if only for a little while. Although ...

'Uncle Sal?'

'Yes, love?'

'You don't think there's trouble between Rob and Lucy, do you? Only it seems so odd for him to leave his family halfway across the country and come down here on his own.'

Uncle Sal gave her an encouraging pat. 'Don't fret about the boy, love. He told us himself that things are pretty tight, and he'd be a fool to turn down a few honest pounds if he can earn them.'

'Yes, but -'

'There is no but, Frances. If you want me to, I'll have a quiet word with your brother, but don't you have to get to work now? It's past noon already.'

'Heavens.' She blew him a kiss as she made for the door. Her boss, Mr Gibbons, had been kind enough to rearrange her shift to accommodate her rehearsals - after all, the show was intended to raise funds for the soup kitchen and the local orphanage which took in more abandoned waifs every day - but she didn't want to be late.

She broke into a trot, catching the tram half a minute before the doors shut. Two pence gone, she thought, but without the urgency she used to feel before Phil and Jack came into their life. They still weren't affluent, by a long shot, but her purse was less strained these days. She'd even set aside two pounds as pocket money for Mum when she went to Melbourne, so her mother could treat herself to something nice.

Frances grabbed the strap dangling from the rail as the tram swayed when it turned around a corner. Rob must feel the pinch pretty badly, too, now that she thought of it. He had looked thin, and his smile had slipped when he felt himself unobserved.

The tram came to a halt, and Frances jumped off.

'Sorry, Clara,' she said as soon as she walked into the telephone exchange.

Her colleague took off her headset and ran her fingers through her frizzy hair, making it stick out in places. 'You sure took your sweet time, Franny,' she said, eyes gleaming with curiosity. 'Did anything happen at the club?'

Frances sat down and arranged her own headset. 'You could say that. My brother turned up out of the blue. That's why I'm late.'

'Oh, how lovely.' Clara lingered, clearly not in a hurry to go home. Poor thing, Frances thought, she didn't have too many pleasures to look forward to, with helping her widowed mother look after five younger siblings. Clara lived for the moments when Frances opened up a bit about the Top Note which to her seemed the pinnacle of high life. She'd never been there. Until now.

Frances angled for her handbag, glad that the lightbulbs that signalled a call stayed resolutely dim. She fished in the bag for an envelope and handed it to Clara.

'For you,' she said. 'Two tickets for the show, dinner and drinks included, courtesy of Uncle Sal and Jack.'

Clara's peaky face took on a pink glow. 'Are you kidding? Two tickets for me?'

'Sure,' Frances said. 'You deserve it, for everything you're doing to help me out here. And anyway, that's what friends are for, right?' That was exaggerating a bit, but it perked Clara up no end.

'Gosh,' she said. 'Thanks, that's spiffing, Fran. Only-', the glow left her face. 'I've got nothing to wear. But thanks anyway.' She put the envelope in Frances's lap. The first lightbulbs began to glow. Drat.

'We'll work out something,' Frances said, as reassuring as she could, covering her mouthpiece with one hand. Clara broke into a hopeful grin and took the envelope again.

Dinner that evening was the most joyous she remembered in a long time. Uncle Sal had phoned Jack and excused themselves, and Mum had thrown herself into a cooking frenzy, judging from the menu. A roast joint, three veg, potatoes and an enormous pavlova for dessert because Rob had always had a sweet tooth. She must have spent the housekeeping money for a whole week on that meal, but Frances decided not to ask any questions.

Rob sat and ate, and Mum watched his every bite

with the solicitude of a mother hen guarding her chick. Frances gave Uncle Sal a quick glance under her lashes. He winked at her.

After the third helping Rob pushed his plate aside. 'Sorry, Mum, I'm full. You're still the best cook in all of Australia, if you ask me.'

'You don't have to flatter me, darling. I only hope you stay long enough for me to get some flesh on your ribs again. You work too hard. I wonder that Lucy didn't say anything.'

'Mum.' He held out his hand to her. 'She said exactly the same thing, and I tell her what I'm telling you now. I'm fine. There's no need to fret over me like I'm an over-grown schoolboy.'

'How is Lucy?' Frances said.

'She's good,' he said. 'Really good. She sends all her love by the way.'

'She must miss you,' Frances said.

'She does. And I miss them. But it can't be helped.' He drummed his fingertips on his glass. 'You see, we're having another baby, and I need every penny I can make.'

'Another little one.' Mum's eyes shone. 'How wonderful. But poor Lucy, to be on her own at such a time.'

'She's not on her own,' Rob said, 'she's back on her parents' farm while I'm away. You don't think I'd leave her alone, do you?' His voice held enough tension to let

Frances have an inkling of how bad he must feel about the situation.

She exchanged a swift glance with Uncle Sal. He got up and said, 'Congratulations, Rob. That calls for a celebration. Maggie, why don't you put your glad rags on while Frances and I clear the table, and then we'll set off to the Top Note. Jack's expecting us at eight.'

Mum clung to Rob's arm all the way to the club, as if he'd slip through her fingers if she let go. Frances and Uncle Sal followed behind as soon as they'd stepped off the tram, to give them some space. Frances was glad Jack hadn't sent the car around as he sometimes did. She didn't want her brother to think of him as flashy.

At the entrance Mum waited for them. Uncle Sal entered with Frances at his side, his head inclined in a small nod to Bluey that conveyed easy familiarity mixed with respect.

Mum handed her coat to Frances's best friend Pauline, who worked as Dolores' Bardon's dresser and doing odd jobs around the club. Pauline's eyes grew huge as she spotted Rob. She clasped a hand to her mouth to stifle a whoopee.

Frances grinned. Pauline never stinted on a dramatically magnified response, thanks to her predilection with actresses like the now out-of-favour

Clara Bow, and she used to have a schoolgirl crush on Rob, ages ago.

Pauline came out from behind the cloakroom counter and stepped up to Rob, an impish smile on her glossy lips. 'Hello, stranger,' she said, just like in the pictures.

'Hello, Pauline,' he said, gazing at her in open amusement. 'You haven't changed a bit.' He gave her a swift peck on the cheek, making her smile even wider. 'Tell Tony from me he's a lucky dog.'

'He'll be disappointed to miss you,' she said. Tony Dixon, her fiancé, was busy doing maintenance on property Jack owned across the city.

'Tell him I'll stick around for a bit.'

They sauntered upstairs to the balcony, to the same table they'd sat at on their first evening at the Top Note, in April. The space only allowed for half a dozen tables, set in niches, and provided privacy coupled with a perfect view of the stage, the dance floor and the bar area downstairs. Blazing chandeliers, wall sconces and mirrors had transformed the lacklustre room. where Frances and Uncle Sal had rehearsed their act this morning, into a palace.

Rob gazed around with the same awe Frances remembered very well. The table was laid with china and crystal, and two silver-plated buckets held corked bottles.

Rob lifted one and whistled through his teeth. 'Champagne? The real thing, I presume?'

'Of course,' said Uncle Sal, secure in his role as a man of the world and almost-host. This was his world, after all. 'Shall we open it?'

'Not before I know what's in the other bottle,' Rob said, winking at Mum.

'It's the Frances Palmer special.' Jack appeared at the head of the staircase. 'Although you probably call it lemonade. Evening, Maggie, Uncle Sal, Frances. If you'd be willing to wait a bit, Dolores will join us after her first set tonight. She's only on for half an hour because we're trying out a new band.'

Rob fingered his tie and shifted around on his seat. He probably felt self-conscious in his blue suit that was shiny with wear, Frances thought, especially when confronted with Jack, who wore his dinner jacket with the same ease as Uncle Sal.

She touched Rob's arm. 'You look great, and you'll adore Dolores,' she said. 'Everybody loves her. Ask Mum if you don't believe me.'

The lights went dim, as search lights hit the stage, illuminating a raven-haired woman dressed in a white satin dress that clung to her every curve. It would have looked cheap on every other woman, thought Frances, but there was nothing vulgar about Dolores Bardon. She glanced at Rob. He stared transfixed at the singer who now crooned 'Stardust' into the microphone. Frances only hoped he wouldn't fall in love with her, now that his wife was far away.

His face still had that dreamy look when Dolores finished her set and walked off-stage.

Mum had to pull his sleeve to get his attention. 'She's wonderful, isn't she? I always make my walnut coffee cake when she comes to visit because it's her favourite. And Phil's.'

Did Mum say that to break Rob's trance and warn him off gently, Frances wondered. Phil Anderson was not only their lodger and Dolores' beau, but also a policeman and as such an authority figure.

Dolores came gliding along, an apparition in black and white, the only bits of colour her crimson lips. She gave Uncle Sal her hand for a kiss and bestowed a dazzling smile on the whole company. 'Frances, darling, you never bring Maggie along often enough. It's been ages, sweetheart.'

She sat down next to Mum, so she faced Rob. Her stockings rustled as she crossed her legs. 'And you must be the famous Rob. Lovely to meet you.'

Rob gazed at her in wonder. 'I'm honoured to meet you, Miss Bardon.'

'Please,' her chocolate eyes twinkled, 'just call me Dolores.'

'Whatever you wish.' He swallowed. Mum frowned a little bit, and Frances suppressed a smile.

How did Dolores do that? She didn't openly flirt with the men, but there was something in her look and her voice that attracted them like honey attracted bluebottles.

Jack rested his hand on her arm. 'Uncle Sal, if you'd open the champagne?' The cork popped with a maximum of noise and no spillage, and Uncle Sal filled the glasses with an added flourish.

'Here's to Rob and happy family reunions,' Jack said as he raised his glass in a toast. 'And I want to bring out a special toast to Uncle Sal. If you'd do me the favour, I'd like to appoint you as artistic director of the Top Note, as well as the show. And before you say yes, that also includes trying to keep all of you guys out of trouble when I'm gone.'

# CHAPTER TWO

*a* chill ran down Frances's spine. She opened her mouth, but no words came out.

Uncle Sal came to her rescue. 'What do you mean, gone? You're not in trouble, are you?'

Frances's hand began to shake. Please no, a voice whispered inside her head. She'd known all along that Jack was breaking the law, selling alcohol after six o'clock, but hardly anyone paid attention to the prohibition, and most of Adelaide's high-ranking councillors and police officers were regulars at the Top Note.

Mum looked as shocked as Frances felt.

Jack chuckled. 'No worries, folks. I'm not on the run. All I'm going to do is make a voyage to New Zealand, to check out the joker my little sister's fallen in love with. I'll be back in less than a fortnight.'

Frances's heart slowed to its usual pace.

'That calls for a toast,' Dolores said. She raised her glass. 'To my darling Rachel. I wish I could go with you, Jack. I haven't seen her for too long.'

'The next time,' he said. 'Remember that sea voyages don't agree with you, and the Tasman can get pretty rough.'

'I know,' Dolores said with a sigh. 'But I miss her so much, and I'd love to see her new fellow.'

'You shall,' Jack said. 'If there are to be wedding bells, you'll be there. As will be others.' He gave Frances a reassuring wink. 'Here's to my sister and to all our loved ones.'

'To family,' Frances said. 'When are you leaving?'

'In four days. Enough time to show Uncle Sal the ropes if he's willing, and to dance with you. Shall we?'

Mum and Rob followed them onto the dance floor.

'I've never seen Maggie this glowing,' Jack said as he pulled Frances close.

'She adores Rob, and she hasn't seen him in such a long time.' Her head barely touched his cheek. 'He does appear strained though, doesn't he? I only hope his new job isn't too hard.'

'What's he going to do exactly?'

'Travelling around the racecourses, looking after the horses.' She paused. 'He'll be alright, won't he?'

'Sure,' Jack said after a heartbeat's pause. 'As long as he steers away from the book-makers. Hard to tell crooks from straight fellows, but surely, he knows all about shady deals at the races. Anyway, a vet's got nothing to do with them.'

'You mean like Phar Lap?' she said, thinking back to a scandal that had rocked Adelaide only last year. 'When he was scratched from the Adelaide Cup at the last moment? Uncle Sal still swears he was nobbled, because no one would bet against him.'

'That's possible. What I do know is that there is a hell of a lot of race fixing going on, in every city. But your brother isn't a jockey who might end up with a broken kneecap if he wins a certain race, so he has nothing to worry about.'

She snuggled closer into his arm. 'Only four more days before you go …'

'I'll be back before you know it, kiddo. You'll be busy enough, with your brother and work and rehearsing your act.' He pushed a lock out of her eyes. 'What's bothering Uncle Sal, by the way?'

'It's his ankle. He says he's too insecure on his feet to do the knife-throwing with me as his target, because he might stumble and lose his aim, and he can't do it sitting down. It's all very frustrating for him.'

'But not as frustrating as skewering you. Well, you'll come up with something.'

She missed a step. 'He wouldn't really hit me, would he?'

'No, Frances, but that's because Uncle Sal knows where to draw the line when it comes to risks.'

'That's true,' she said. 'But still, I hate to see him so disappointed.'

The music stopped and he led her back to the table.

Rob and Mum arrived one song later. Mum looked flushed, but happy. 'That was wonderful,' she said. 'You're just as good a dancer as your dad was.'

'Only with the right partner,' he said. 'I hope we can do that again, sometime soon. But now I'd better get some sleep if I want to be any good tomorrow morning. I've been up since four.'

'Why didn't you say so?' Mum said. 'We could have had a quiet evening at home.'

'And miss a swell party like this, with you and my little sister?'

'Well, that's true. Won't you at least sleep at home tonight, and I'll make you your favourite breakfast in the morning?'

Frances and Uncle Sal exchanged an amused glance. It would be hard for Rob to make his escape.

'I'm sorry,' he said. 'But I don't want to jeopardise my job, Mum. My employers don't know I've got family down here. They like their people to be independent, without folks who hang around, looking for dead certs or inside tips.'

A note of embarrassment crept into his voice. 'I don't mean you, but, well, that's how it is. You understand, right?'

'Sure, my darling.' Mum took his hand. 'But you'll be allowed to see us sometimes?'

'He will,' Frances said. 'You haven't enlisted in the army, have you? And even they have leave until curfew.'

They all got up.

'I'll be around so much you'll tell me to get out of your hair, Mum,' Rob said. 'Miss Dolores, Jack, thanks for a spiffing evening.'

'My pleasure,' said Jack. 'I'll see you soon. When's the next rehearsal, Uncle Sal? Tomorrow? Maybe you could stay on afterwards.'

'Sure.'

Dolores blew him a kiss. 'Bye, darlings. Bluey will take you home.'

It took Rob less than five minutes to arrange his few belongings in the small room next to the jockey school. A brass bedstead covered with a rough blanket, a scarred chest of drawers with a wobbly leg and a metal chair took up most of the space. He set the framed picture of Lucy and Rob Jnr on top of the chest and lay down on the bed, looking at his wife's smiling face. He missed her so much it hurt. And his boy. He'd only been on the road for three weeks, and already he'd missed his son's first steps.

Loud snores penetrated his ears. If Brocky, the blacksmith they'd put next to him, kept this racket on, there was no hope of sleep. A burly fellow, big enough to hold any horse single-handedly. Odd; he'd met Brocky first a week ago at Yarra Glen racecourse, and the blacksmith had told him he never steered further away than a hundred miles in each direction. When they'd met here at the wash house, Brocky had greeted him with a resounding smack on the back and a genuine smile.

Rob wondered briefly if the other man had left his family behind as well. He'd had a lonesome look in his eyes when he said that he didn't know a single soul in Adelaide.

The snores changed their rhythm. It was almost a tune, thought Rob, although one he wouldn't care to dance to. It had been great to see Mum, and Frances, and Uncle Sal. And Miss Dolores – any man would be hard pressed to keep his eyes off her. He only hoped that Jack fellow wouldn't let her turn his head and hurt Frances. But no. Uncle Sal trusted the man, so he was okay in his book. Still, that singer was something.

Rob's glance wandered towards Lucy's photo. He didn't need it to remind him of the way she looked, or how her red hair curled around her face. She wasn't a beauty like Miss Dolores, but he wouldn't trade places with any man in the world. No one in the whole world could touch his Lucy. Tomorrow he'd write her a long letter and tell her about the family.

What he wouldn't tell her was that he'd come close to giving in to having the lads place a bet for him. 'No-one will know, mate,' the sandy-haired jockey had said. 'She's a sweet little runner, this mare. Odds of ten to one, too.' He'd rustled two one-pound notes before Rob's ears.

'Sorry,' Rob had said. 'Can't do that. I'm not allowed with me being the vet here.'

'Sure?' The jockey had shrugged and walked off. And confound it, if the mare hadn't come first. Ten to one – two pounds would have brought in more than most fellows earned in a whole month.

No, he couldn't tell Lucy that, especially not how tempted he'd really been. That one bet would have paid enough to buy everything Lucy needed for Rob Jnr and the new baby.

He turned down the kerosene lamp and drifted off into sleep to the accompaniment of Brocky's snoring.

Frances lay awake until long after midnight. Thoughts chased each other in her mind. A fortnight without Jack – and hadn't she heard something about how easily romance blossomed on board of a ship? And which girl wouldn't find him attractive, with his easy confidence, broad shoulders, and the humour and intelligence in his sleepy eyes?

But she could trust him, couldn't she? Just like Lucy could trust Rob. It was too bad that her brother had to leave them, but on the other hand it was nice to have him back for a while. And he'd always loved horses, so this was perfect for him.

She wondered if he'd have time to attend the charity show. She'd be dazzling in the limelight, with thousands of sparks being reflected in the sequins of her dress, and the glittery eyeshadow that would make her look like a movie star.

She'd come up with something to let Uncle Sal show everyone that he was still Salvatore the Magnificent, and who knew, there might be a photograph of them in The Advertiser, and a paragraph about how he and Miss Francesca had stolen the show ...

The whole next day she still felt as if she was floating on air. Her happiness wasn't hurt by the fact that she saw several young men follow her with appreciative glances as she walked to work.

She used her lunch break for one of her favourite tasks, drawing up a list of pleasurable things to do. She wrote down Clara in nice big letters. Her workmate deserved a treat; whenever she'd asked Frances about her life, she'd done so without any rancour or reservations, happy enough to get a glimpse of a life beyond her own straitened circumstances. Poor Clara, she'd never be pretty with her thin, frizzy hair and pasty skin, but Frances jolly well intended to try.

She tapped at her lips with the end of the pencil. Pauline was a wiz when it came to beauty, and she'd be delighted to help. But what about a dress? Frances ran through her own restricted wardrobe in her mind, but where she tended to be curvier than the current fashion, Clara was boyish to the extreme.

She wrote down, hair and face, Pauline, dress?

What next? Of course, the variety show tickets for the O'Leary sisters who sold used clothes in their cramped shop around the corner. They were old friends, two spinsters whose kind hearts sometimes overruled their sharp minds.

Frances chuckled to herself. All she had to do was to hand them the invitations and mention Clara's plight. They'd be sure to let her borrow a dress. Their names went next on the list. Now all she needed to sort out was Uncle Sal's predicament.

The first lightbulb flashed. Frances pushed the list aside and returned to her duties.

When she left the telephone exchange, she found Jack waiting for her at the back door. The warm feeling inside her stomach that always appeared when she saw him spread until it reached her toes. It was an odd sensation that hadn't lessened in the six months she had known him. She wondered if he felt the same, or if it was a girlish thing.

'Hi kiddo,' he said, giving her a crooked smile.

'What a lovely surprise,' she said, feeling her lips curl up at their own accord.

'I'm not needed for a few hours, so I thought we'd make the most of it before I'm off. Bluey's holding the fort for me, giving Uncle Sal the grand tour.'

He took her arm. 'Shall I take you home, or shall we

watch the latest show at the Empire? We've missed the first part of the double-bill, but I seem to remember that you wanted to see the main picture.'

'Yes, please,' she said. 'That is, I'd like to phone up Mum first and ask her if she knows if Rob'll be around tonight.'

'Sure, although I doubt if he'll have an evening off soon,' he said, leading her to the telephone kiosk on King William Street. 'The racing business doesn't conform to normal office hours.'

It still gave her a thrill to dial her own phone number. At first, she'd worried about the expense of such a luxury as a telephone, but now she couldn't imagine life without it. Apart from being indispensable to their police officer lodger, Dolores' beau Phil, it also afforded her the freedom to stay out whenever she, or rather Jack, felt like it, without having Mum worry herself to a frazzle about where she was.

'Mum?' she asked. 'Have you heard from Rob yet?'

'No,' said Mum. 'He'll be way too busy.'

'Right-ho. I just wanted to say I'll be to the pictures with Jack. I'll be home for dinner.'

'Fine. Have fun, love.'

The girl in the ticket kiosk treated Frances to a conspiratorial wink as she handed her the tickets while Jack went to the rest room. 'I haven't seen you two lovebirds in a while,' she said. 'Enjoy the show. It's ever so lovely.'

Frances smiled at her. 'We will. Thanks.' Funny how she no longer blushed, when someone talked about her private life. But they'd been here so often the girl was almost an old acquaintance, and anyway there had been no-one else close by.

The picture was every bit as hilarious as Frances had hoped. 'Palmy Days' had been announced as one of the biggest hits of the year, with Eddie Cantor playing the patsy for a fortune-teller who planned to make off with the payroll money from a bakery.

The best part though was the dancing, with a line–up of the famous Goldwyn girls tapping and whirling their way from bakery to gymnasium in breath-taking speed. Their dresses alone beguiled Frances. She risked a sideways glance at Jack to see how he felt about all the female beauty showing off perfect legs and more cleavage than she could offer. Instead, she found him looking at her. She snuggled back against his shoulder until the curtain came down.

'Thank you, Jack,' she said as they left the Empire. 'Did you enjoy it as much as I did?'

'As long as it's with you, I'd enjoy anything.'

She laughed. 'Well, at least it should have given you some ideas for the variety show at the club, right?'

'You mean I should hire the Goldwyn girls? Bit out of my league, I'm afraid, and the geography doesn't work at all.'

She squeezed his arm. 'Very funny, but you haven't got a proper dance act lined up yet, do you?'

'That's true. What about you and Pauline? You'd make a lovely duo.'

'Signorina Francesca is busy enough, thank you very much. Although Pauline is great on roller skates. We used to go down to the rink all the time.'

A thought formed in her head. 'Jack?'

'Yes?'

'What if Uncle Sal sits on a bar stool, one that is fastened onto a small turn-table, so Uncle Sal can sit with his good leg on the ground, and someone on roller skates twirls him around when he throws the knives? That might give him the speed and the movement in his upper body he needs.'

He pulled her close and dropped a kiss on her hair. 'That's my girl. We'd have to ask him, but it sounds good to me. Come on, he should still be at the Top Note.'

'Yes,' Uncle Sal said, when she explained her idea to him in the smoke-filled back room where the props were stored.

He'd rehearsed without her today, and tiredness deepened the lines fanning out from his eyes like a spider web. But his evening clothes were as dapper as they could be, and his silver-shot black hair remained unruffled. He'd always come alive in the presence of a stage, Frances realised. They'd have to make the plan work, for his sake.

He stroked his chin. 'The only thing is, who'll push me around when I'm throwing my knives at you? You can't do both, and Pauline, bless her heart, will have more than enough to do backstage, doing hair and make-up.'

They both looked at Jack. He raised his hands, palms outwards. 'Don't ask me,' he said. 'That is, unless...'

'Yes?'

'What about Marie? Bluey's been feeling pretty bad about her having to stay at home with the kids and missing all the fun.'

'That's a bonzer idea. Shall we ask Bluey straight away?' Jack's right-hand man adored his headstrong wife, and so did everyone else.

'Sure. He'll take you two home now anyway. You can ask him then,' Jack said. 'And now I'll have to leave you. I still have a few things to do.'

He blew her a kiss as he walked to the door. 'By the way,' he said, 'you do have Saturday off, don't you?'

'Yes. And Sunday.'

'Sunday's too late for me, because my ship departs in the wee hours, but how about I take you and Uncle Sal to the races on Saturday? We won't be able to see your brother, but at least you'll get a feeling for his new work sphere.'

'Good-oh,' said Uncle Sal, rubbing his hands. 'I've got a hunch I might have a light flutter if there's a dappled

31

grey running. They never lost me any money yet, dappled greys. But we better don't tell Maggie. She disapproves of gambling.'

'No worries, Uncle Sal. Haven't you forgotten that she leaves on Saturday on the midday train?'

Uncle Sal's eyes lit up. 'Great. We'll miss her, of course, but, well, there's no denying even she does have her shortcomings, great gal that she is.'

Mum left in a flurry of last-minute instructions on who of the neighbours to look after, the number of casseroles and stews she'd prepared or had been promised by friends, and when to expect her phone call. Thanks to the fact that Rob had been able to spare her a couple of hours on Thursday morning while Frances was at work, Mum set off with a beaming smile.

She clutched her train ticket in a gloved hand while Frances searched for the reserved seat in the second-class coach. She'd insisted on leaving the packed sandwiches that her mother had intended for her dinner, at home.

'Do you see that?' Frances pointed to a carriage with red velvet curtains draping the windows. 'It's the dining car, and I've made a reservation for you for the 6.30 dinner.'

'But that must be horrifically expensive,' Mum said, her brows divided by a big crease.

'It's already paid for, and everything is included.' Frances opened the door to Mum's carriage and ushered her inside. Two of the four seats were already taken, by an elderly priest and a woman who looked similar enough to be his sister. She peered at Mum with short-sighted eyes, her hands smoothing her skirt.

'Good day,' said Mum as she sat down.

Frances stored the suitcase on the overhead rack and bent down to kiss Mum's cheek. 'Bye, darling mother, and don't forget to enjoy yourself. This is your holiday, remember? And give my love to Uncle Fred and Aunt Milly.'

She dashed off after one last fond look at her mother. Half an hour to get home and get ready for the races! She hadn't mentioned that trip to her mother at all, although her conscience gave her a brief prick.

Uncle Sal waited at the station exit. 'Well, love,' he said as they boarded the tram, 'now it's just the two of us. We'll be fine, eh?'

'Absolutely,' she said, although it did feel funny to have a whole month ahead, without Mum fussing over them. Phil must have felt the same, because he'd offered to move out while Mum was away, to keep propriety. Silly, but sweet. As if anybody could get the wrong idea, with Uncle Sal around.

'Should we ask Phil if he wants to come along too, with Dolores?' she asked.

Uncle Sal snorted. 'Better not. You don't turn up at the racecourse with the police in tow, love. People get funny ideas, and you don't want them to get the wrong impression about Rob, in case someone makes the connection?'

Her cheeks grew warm. 'But he isn't doing anything wrong.'

'Of course not. But you know, some people get kind of nervous when there's police around. Especially where money flows.' The tram swerved, and Uncle Sal nearly lost his balance. His jaw clenched as he grabbed the leather strap dangling from the ceiling.

Sometimes he walked painlessly, with barely a limp, but today the air had the soggy feel of a sweaty towel, and that caused him problems.

'What should I wear?' she asked as they entered the house.

'Something pretty but not fancy,' he said. 'It can be a mite dusty, and there's bound to be a throng at the grand-stand.'

'Right-ho,' she said, as she rushed upstairs, taking two steps at once.

Jack rang at the door two minutes after she'd come down, freshly powdered and with a slick of lipstick on her mouth. Her yellow jumper and emerald skirt had seen better days, but the colours suited her.

Uncle Sal took off his hat like he always did as she entered the room. 'Shall we, Signorina Francesca?'

She slid her arm through his. 'With the greatest pleasure, gentlemen.'

The crowd and the noise at Morphettville were much bigger than she'd expected. Nattily dressed men rubbed shoulders with veterans in ill-fitting suits, urchins running errands, housewives on the search for a thrill and heavily made-up girls who tried to keep the attention of their male friends over the attractions of the bookies.

Jack nodded left and right as he secured them a way to the seats on the covered stand. 'You two stay here,' he said after they'd sat down. 'I'll get a racing programme and refreshments. Lemonade for you, kiddo, and beer for us, Uncle Sal?'

Uncle Sal chuckled as he watched Frances open astonishment. 'This isn't busy, love, just a nice turn-out. Nothing wrong with it, if you keep your head and don't get carried away. Now my Dad, he always swore he'd inherited his horse-sense from his grandfather, an Italian grandee. Blow me if he didn't fall for every three-legged mare that ever set its hooves on the turf. He reckoned if they did come in, they'd come in big.' He tapped his nose. 'Never ever believe that a horse will make your luck, and you'll be fine. Especially if it's a dappled grey you're betting on.'

Frances leant forward, watching the line-up of horses who got ready for the next race. 'I like the black one,' she said, 'with the gold and green colours.'

'That's good to hear,' Jack said, reappearing with a

rolled-up paper under his arm and two pitchers. Cups were in his pockets. 'I've put a guinea on that mare.' He put the pitchers down in front of them.

'I didn't expect you so soon,' said Uncle Sal as he took the paper and opened it. 'You must have run into lots of mates, eh?'

'Some,' Jack said. 'Anyway, whoever wants to talk to me knows where to find me. Most people asked about our show and Dolores.'

Frances fanned her face. The sun bleached the sky almost white. A shot rang out, and the crowd roared as the horses streaked out of their starting gates. Her heart pounded in her ears as the black mare inched her way from second to last to runner-up position.

'Come on,' she yelled in unison with Uncle Sal, gripped by a feverish desire to see the horse win.

The mare stretched her neck longer, as if she'd heard Frances, throwing up a cloud of dust with every step.

The jockey in the lead began to whip the neck of his horse in a frantic rhythm.

The black mare strained so hard that white foam dripped from her mouth. Half a length separated her from the number one, a quarter length, now they were neck to neck …

'Oh, yes,' Frances said, her mouth dry with excitement. Less than a hand was between the leading horses as the mare made a final effort and crossed the finish.

Jack pressed a filled cup into her hand.

'She deserved to win.'

'She sure did, kiddo. That was a great race.' He tapped the pocket with his ticket. 'A win of six shillings for us. Who shall we put that money on?'

Two hours later, Jack and Frances had pocketed six pounds between them, and Uncle Sal's fondness of greys had netted him a handsome tenner.

Frances sighed as they made their way to the exit. She'd have liked to stay longer, but Jack needed to get home. She shaded her eyes to get one last good look at the horses, as the winner of the last race, a nondescript brown horse, was led to the blacksmith because it had lost a shoe when it came off the track.

The blacksmith signalled a slight boy of about fourteen to hold the horse while he lifted the hoof.

'Bloody hell!' he said, his mouth gaping wide. He let go of the horse's leg. 'I know this gelding, and if he's a novice racer, I'm the bloody queen of the fairies.'

'Damn,' Jack said, steering Frances and Uncle Sal towards the exit as fast as he could.

A throng of men surrounded the blacksmith, who backed against the wall of the stable building, squaring his shoulders.

'What's going on?' said Frances as soon as they'd reached the car. She heard shouts from outside, although she couldn't make out the words.

'Trouble,' said Jack. 'A hell of a lot of trouble. But nothing to do with Rob, if that's what you're afraid of.'

# CHAPTER THREE

'What would you like to do now?' Jack asked as he turned the car in the direction of the city centre. 'I've got a couple of urgent things to attend to, so if you don't want to come along, I'll drop you off at home. Otherwise Bluey will do that later.'

'I'd love to come,' Frances said, intent on spending as much time with Jack as she could before he left. 'What about you, Uncle Sal?'

'What kind of a silly question is that?' he said, smoothing the pencil-thin moustache he'd grown for his stage comeback. 'Don't forget I'm your chaperon. Where you go, I go, especially when there's music and champagne involved.'

Frances caught the exchange of a quick glance between Jack and Uncle Sal in the rear-view mirror. Something was out of kilter here. Or maybe it just felt like that, because of Jack's leaving and Uncle Sal's taking charge.

'Don't forget, my boy, tonight I'm paying,' Uncle Sal said. He patted the pocket that held his winnings. 'Do we know how to pick them, eh?'

'Do you know if Phil's going to be around tonight?' Jack said after a moment's pause. 'I haven't seen him in a while. It'd be nice to say good-bye.'

'Phil? Oh, right. Yeah, I think he mentioned something. He's been pretty busy lately.'

'That's true. Mum practically had to waylay him so she could introduce him to Rob, and even then, he was off again after a few minutes,' Frances said. 'But you could always ring him up.' She turned her head to face Uncle Sal. 'When does Mum's train arrive in Melbourne? We'd better be home when she phones us.'

'Her train's due in an hour, and I said we'd phone her, so the expense won't fall on your Uncle Fred,' Uncle Sal said. 'I hope you don't mind, Jack. I'll pay you back, of course.'

The sun had barely set, but preparations for the night's revel were already under way. Soft sounds filtered through the rooms, with the band warming up for their performance. Snowy cloth covered the tables, and the thick carpet showed spotless in the light of the chandeliers.

No matter how often she'd seen it, Frances still marvelled at the change from the smoke-filled, alcohol-soaked dancehall the club became in the early hours to

39

sweet-smelling, pristine freshness. The two faces of the Top Note, she thought. 'It's like day and night, isn't it?'

'Eh?' Uncle Sal gazed around with narrow eyes, obviously lost in his own world. 'You two go ahead,' he said, 'and don't mind me. I've got an idea or two I'd like to play around with.' Without waiting for a reply, he made for the stage which for now was bare except for a drum-set and a baby grand piano.

Frances smiled. Like the club, Uncle Sal also had different sides to him. It took a lot of imagination to reconcile the dapper vaudeville artist with the slight man in a patched cardigan and an apron, doing the dishes with her or peeling vegetables for Mum.

'Are you coming?' Jack asked.

'Sorry, I was wool-gathering.' She smiled at him. How many faces had Jack, she wondered? He could be tough, ruthless, but he was also the most caring man she'd ever known, as evidenced by the assembled staff of his club, all of which had bonds together going back to the Great War.

He winked at her, and her smile widened. He was also the most attractive man she'd ever known.

'You look very pensive,' he said as he opened the door to his apartment on the second floor.

'I've just been wondering if I really know you,' she said, following him inside. 'Or rather, how many of your faces I know. '

'And?'

'I can't say. I can't even say how many of Uncle Sal's faces I know.'

'What about yourself?'

'Me? That's easy. I'm just plain old Frances Palmer, that's all there is to me.' She couldn't help but feel a pang of frustration.

Jack opened the door to his fridge and took out a pitcher of iced water. He filled two glasses and handed her one.

'That's what you say,' he said, curling a lock of her hair around his finger. 'What about the girl who supports her family and friends every which way, who flaunts convention by asking for lemonade in a night-club and going out with a sly-grogger? And what about Signorina Francesca, who is as fearless as she is beautiful, offering herself to have knives flung at her?'

The breath caught in her throat. 'Beautiful?'

'To me you are, sweetheart. Always.'

'You never said that before.'

'No.'

There was a question in his eyes, and an invitation. He put down his glass and took her face in both hands. 'Frances, I know this is probably bad timing, but ...'

Three rapid raps on the door interrupted them.

Frances could have howled with frustration as Jack released her to open the door to Bluey.

'Sorry to disturb you, Mr Jack,' he said, as normally placid face screwed up. 'The man in the valley's tried to pull

41

one on us again. Half his delivery is watered down so much you could bottle-feed it to a baby. The rest of the wine seems fine.' He shook his head. 'Can't trust anyone these days.'

Jack raked his fingers through his hair. 'Sorry, sweetheart, I need to sort this out. This might take a bit. Will I see you downstairs when I'm done, or would you like to see Dolores, if you still don't mind waiting?'

'I'd love to see her, if she's not too busy.'

She tapped on the door to the second apartment.

'Coming,' Dolores' mellow voice rang out. She flung the door open and enveloped Frances in a cloud of silk kimono and Chanel No 5. 'I was hoping you'd drop in, darling. Do sit down, will you, while I get changed? Oh, and if you'd like a drink, you know where everything is.'

Frances sank into a black leather armchair, Dolores' latest acquisition. The whole sitting room looked like in the glossy magazines the singer adored, she thought, with its black and chrome furniture and the glass table. The only spots of colour drawing the eye came in the form of a mass of red roses that adorned the mantel.

Dolores wafted out of her bedroom, dressed in a clinging black frock that accentuated the whiteness of her skin. She curled up on the settee opposite Frances and sighed. 'Hard to believe he'll be gone in the morning. It's silly, but things simply won't feel the same.'

42

'No,' Frances said. A lump formed in her throat. 'Still, it won't be for too long.'

'Unless he doesn't like Rachel's new beau and has to prise her from him.' Dolores' dark eyes grew troubled. 'Do they have crooks on New Zealand sheep stations? She wouldn't fall for another bad lot, would she?'

'Of course not,' said Frances, more to reassure Dolores than from conviction. After all, she'd never met Jack's younger sister whom he'd rescued from the clutches of a cocaine dealer. 'Isn't she living with family anyway? They're bound to take a good look at any man in her life.'

'Like Uncle Sal did with Jack?' Dolores' angled for the water glass sitting on the side table and took a deep sip. 'No need to blush, darling. I think it's sweet, the way he watches over you.'

'Well, I mean ...'

'Funny should Rachel get married first.' Dolores gave her an impish smile. 'Has he proposed yet, or is he still doing his strong restrained act?'

Frances shook her head. Honestly, Dolores could be impossible, but she couldn't bring herself to feel vexed about this intrusion into her private life. Especially not since this was what she'd wanted to hear all along, that Jack cared as much for her as she did for him. Still, no need to show it too obviously. 'He hasn't said anything, but why should he?'

'Men.' Dolores' rolled her eyes heavenwards. 'There all the same, brave as what have you in the war, and too scared in real life to utter a few words. Unless – you wouldn't reject him, would you? I don't think he could go through that again.'

Frances's mouth fell open.

Dolores said, 'Hasn't he told you? He was as good as engaged once, when he had his pockets full of money from his mining days, but then the trouble with Rachel broke, and little dearie figured that Jack came with a lot of baggage and more than a few mouths to feed, so she split and hooked herself up with a wallet on legs.' She snorted. 'Everyone but Jack knew she was nothing but a common gold-digger, but he fell for it.'

'That must have been bad.'

'Yes, especially on top of everything else. You won't tell him that I told you, though, darling? I don't want to hurt his feelings.'

'I promise.'

'Good-oh.' She glanced at the clock on the mantel. 'Heavens, Pauline should be here any minute to do my hair. You're staying for my set, aren't you? And where's Uncle Sal, by the way? I've got a fabulous idea for our show that I can't wait to run past my new artistic director.'

'He's downstairs, probably examining the stage from every angle. I'd better join him, after I've rung up Mum in Melbourne.'

'Feel free to use my telephone, darling, and give Maggie my love.' Dolores blew her a kiss as she opened the door for Pauline.

Frances fished the paper with Uncle Fred's phone number out of her skirt pocket. It felt strange to give an operator the number she wanted, instead of sitting at the switchboard herself.

Mum must have waited by the telephone, because she was on the line without delay. 'How are you, love?' she said.

'Fine,' Frances said. 'And you? Did you have a good journey?'

'Marvellous, but I wish I could have had more time with Rob.'

'Never mind,' said Frances. 'Don't forget he's got two days between racecourses when you're back.'

'That's true. And it is nice to see Fred und Millie, after all this time. They're taking me out to dinner tomorrow.' Mum spoke faster, obviously mindful of the expense. 'And Frances, tell Uncle Sal to keep an eye on Rob, will you?'

'He'll be fine, Mum. Now, you take care of you, and I'll ring you up again next weekend. Oh, and Dolores and Jack send their love. Bye.'

She strolled downstairs, deep in thought. A broken engagement – she should have guessed that long ago. How anyone could dump Jack because he would always be there for the people he cared about, was beyond her. She must have been very pretty, that girl, for a sophisticated man like Jack to fall in love with her.

She mentally slapped herself. This was all in the past, and hadn't he called her beautiful only today?

She'd be stupid to let old stories bother her, and if Dolores believed that Jack was in love with Frances Palmer, well ... A warm feeling crept up in her stomach.

Three hours later, after Dolores' performance and a relaxed dinner with her and Uncle Sal, now and then interrupted by Jack who only managed to drop by for a few minutes at a time, she found herself alone with Jack for the last time before his trip.

He hugged her close.

She clung to the lapels of his dinner jacket.

'Take care, sweetheart,' he said. 'I'm sorry I didn't have time to talk to you today, but we'll make up for that when I'll come home, sweetheart.'

'As long as you do return.' She inhaled the mixture of spicy toilet water and sun-warmed skin that for her was the essence of Jack.

'I'll always come back to you.' He bent to kiss her. She melted into his arms.

She was still short of breath, five minutes later, when Bluey ushered her and Uncle Sal into the car to drive them home.

The kitchen seemed empty without Mum. Normally on a Sunday morning, especially when Frances had a day off, the smell of fresh coffee and sizzling bacon would greet her. Today, it was the sight of used dishes in the sink and a drooping geranium on the window sill.

She frowned. Usually Phil could be relied upon to clean up after himself. But these days he seemed to be always in a rush, which could only mean that his police department investigated a serious case. She put the kettle on. Only a quarter to eight, but she had been unable to sleep longer. By now Jack's boat would be out in the open sea.

Hurried steps on the staircase, followed by more measured alerted her to the present. She took butter and bacon out of the refrigerator and reached for Mum's apron.

'Morning, Frances, Uncle Sal.' Phil's eyes were bloodshot, and a trickle of blood oozed from a tiny shaving cut on his left cheek. 'Sorry about the mess. How's Maggie?'

'Everything's good with us,' she said, putting the frying pan on. 'But what's the matter with you? You look terrible?'

'You know I can't tell you,' he said, rubbing his eyes.

Uncle Sal peered at him. 'When did you last have a proper meal, mate?'

'Wednesday. I think.'

Frances shook her head and cracked six eggs into the pan. They'd have a proper Sunday breakfast, even without Mum, and then she and Uncle Sal would practice their juggling act in the garden.

'We missed you last night,' Uncle Sal said. 'Or did you drop in at the Top Note after we'd left?'

'No. I'm sorry I missed Jack, but lately it's been one thing after another. I hoped I'd catch you in the afternoon, but you were gone.'

Frances slid bacon into the pan. 'Jack took us to the races.' She grinned. 'I'm not asking Uncle Sal to tell you his secret, but you won't believe how much fun it is. I picked three winners!'

'Beginners' luck,' Uncle Sal said. 'Don't get too excited. A little flutter is all very well, but it doesn't do to get too keen on playing the ponies.'

'As if I would.'

Frances waited patiently until the bacon was nice and crispy before she distributed eggs and bacon evenly on the plates. They ate in silence, only interrupted by the ticking of the wall clock and the scraping of cutlery on china.

Phil had just emptied his third cup of coffee when Uncle Sal said, 'There was a bit of a to-do yesterday, after the novices' race. Probably nothing to it, but still, I thought you might like to know.'

'The blacksmith, right? We heard about it already. I'm going out there before the meeting starts this afternoon, to have a quiet word with the fellow, and with the racecourse manager and his assistant. Poor fellows, having to deal with this.'

'You're not going to talk to Rob, are you?' Frances said.

'There's no reason why I should. There won't be anything in it at all, believe me. You can forget about it.'

~

The day grew as hot as the day before. At lunch time they decided to stop juggling oranges, balls and, in Uncle Sal's case, three jewel-hilted daggers, and go to Elder park with its shady trees and lake for swimming.

They came home to an empty house in the evening, sandy and tired.

'Thank you for a spiffing day, Uncle Sal,' Frances said as they parted for the night.

He ruffled her hair. 'Anytime, love. Anytime. You're on an early shift tomorrow, right? Then I'll meet you after work at the club.'

~

Frances was busy at work when her colleague Clara tiptoed into the telephone exchange and whispered into her ear. 'I think you'd better go at once. Your Uncle Sal's waiting outside, and he's all horrible and grey in his face.'

'Oh no.' Frances tore off her headset. 'Thanks, Clara.' She rushed out the door. Apart from the damaged ankle as the result of being hit by a drunken driver, Uncle Sal was as fit as a fiddle. Her throat constricted.

'Frances?' He really looked ashen, and his breathing was shallow.

Tears welled up in her eyes. 'What are you doing here? You're ill. You should be at the doctor's.' She clasped his sleeve. 'Come on, we'll get a taxi.'

'Wait, love. I've got bad news.'

Black spots appeared in front of her eyes. 'It's Jack, isn't it? The boat sank, right, just like the *Titanic*? But there are no ice-bergs on the way to New Zealand.' She was babbling now. Sweat formed on her forehead.

Uncle Sal hugged her. 'Calm down, Frances. Jack's alright. It's Rob. Phil called me. The blacksmith has been murdered, and the police have arrested your brother.'

# CHAPTER FOUR

*R*ob sat hunched at the back of the holding cell. His head should be bursting with unanswered question, but it wasn't. His brain was numb. His whole body was, except for his left arm that one of the policemen had twisted on his back to handcuff him. The cell stank of stale tobacco smoke and fear. How many men had sat here before him, drenched in sweat, dreading what was to come? A wave of nausea washed over him. He forced it down; wasn't any sign of weakness considered to be a sign of guilt?

In the cell next to his, a man shouted obscenities.

'Hold it, mate,' the guard yelled as he walked past Rob. 'You keep your ugly gob shut, you hear me? Lor', why do you jokers always end up with me instead of in the drunk-tank where you belong.' He came back and peered at Rob. 'You all right there? Want me to get you some water?'

'Yes, please.' How long had been sitting here? Hours? He couldn't tell. All he knew that they had come for him in the morning, while he attended to a colicky gelding. He'd been called out shortly past midnight. The horse, a promising three-year-old, rolled around in his box, foam flecking his mouth and running down his neck. The heartbeat was erratic and the body temperature climbing.

An eternity later, Rob dimly remembered shouting outside the box, something about Brocky, but he hadn't paid attention. Nothing mattered apart from the horse. He'd called for more helpers, to force the horse up onto his legs before he ruptured his bowel, and to lead him into the arena.

Two stable hands – God, he couldn't even remember their names, let alone their faces - held the trembling horse, while he fished around in his medical bag for the big syringe. He couldn't find it, or the vial with tranquiliser, so he used a smaller syringe instead. Gradually the horse's spasm had eased, and his breath grew stronger.

He'd dismissed one of the stable hands, relying on the other man to help him rub the gelding dry while walking him around, always waiting for the first steaming load of manure which surely must come now any minute.

The commotion outside had grown worse, as a number of men trampled through, regardless of disturbing the horses with their clanging boots and raised voices. The gelding had just relieved himself with a groan, when three men entered, telling him he was under arrest. He barely had time to give the stable hand further instructions for the horse's treatment before he found himself handcuffed and bundled off into a van.

'Here's your water, mate.' The guard pushed a cup into Rob's hand, looking at him in the detached manner of someone who's seen it all before without anything leaving its mark.

Not overly bright, Rob thought, but also not hostile. He managed a weak smile. 'Thank you.'

'No worries.' The guard turned on his heel.

'Excuse me,' Rob said. 'What's going to happen now?'

'Not been here before, have you? You just wait and sit tight until someone comes for you.' The guard guffawed at his joke.

Rob drained his cup in three gulps. Lucy! What would they tell her? He banged his cup against the concrete wall. 'Excuse me, officer?'

A chair scraped across the floor. The guard shuffled close. 'Yeah?'

'My wife,' Rob said, 'it's only – should anyone call my wife, please break it to her gently. She's – she's expecting.'

A kind gleam shone in the officer's eyes. 'Right-ho.' He gave Rob an encouraging nod.

'And if there's any way to remind the stable hand that the horse needs to be walked for a bit longer, and to make sure he does only get a small amount of water to drink? The water mustn't be too cold.'

'Yeah, and while you're at it, bring me a cold beer and scratch my bum, will ya, 'cause I got me an itch,' the man in the neighbouring cell yelled.

The guard raised a fist. 'I've had it up to here with you, matey. You got any more things to say, you tell 'em to our sergeant. He'll cool your itch for you alright.' He gave Rob a thumbs up.

Rob expelled his breath. He'd have to put his faith in the man. Or in Mum's lodger. He'd caught a glimpse of Phil Anderson when they brought him in, but Phil had quickly looked the other way. Still, at least there was someone he knew. Uncle Sal and Frances would soon enough find out what had happened to him.

A sob rose in his throat. What exactly had happened? Thus far he hadn't been told what he was accused of.

# CHAPTER FIVE

'What is Rob accused of?' Frances clung to her sanity with all her might. Uncle Sal had taken her home straight away, after that first horrible moment at the phone exchange. He'd insisted she sit down on the sofa and put her feet up, while he made a pot of tea.

Uncle Sal pulled a leather-covered flask out of his cardigan pocket and poured them both a small amount of brandy. 'Murder,' he said, sitting down next to her.

She closed her eyes. 'No. That's impossible.'

'I know that, love, and you know that. The police don't. All they have to work with is a dead blacksmith who ended up with a bashed-in head after recognising a novice horse as a former winner. That's mighty fishy alright.'

'But what's Rob got to do with it?'

'I can't tell you that, love.' He smoothed back her hair

and took her face in his hands. 'Phil will tell us soon enough. We'll just have to wait for him.'

'Phil! Of course. He can help us.' She sank against Uncle Sal's shoulder. 'If only Jack were here.'

'He'll soon be back. On more day, and you can phone him up in New Zealand.' He rocked her like a small child. 'All we have to do is keep our wits about us and everything will be fine.'

She attempted a smile. 'Can I have another brandy?'

'A wee tot,' he said. 'But first we need to ring up your mum before she reads the paper.'

'Oh my God. Do you think there will be articles about the murder outside of Adelaide? We have to break it to Lucy.'

'Let's leave that to your mum, love.' He patted her hand. His usually sparkling brown eyes had clouded over with concern.

She pressed his hand. 'What do I say?'

'The truth. That there's been a murder at the racecourse, Rob is implied, but he'll soon enough be cleared. Maggie's the daughter and sister of policemen, Frances. She'll trust in the course of justice.'

Uncle Sal was right, Mum had taken it better than expected, and she had promised to phone up Lucy with the horrible news. Better yet, instead of insisting on rushing back to be at Rob's side she'd let herself be convinced that, if she didn't want to stay put, Lucy and Rob Jnr would need her most.

Frances's stomach rumbled. Darkness set in fast, and still no sign of Phil. 'He isn't avoiding us, is he?' she asked Uncle Sal.

'Who, Phil? Why should he? You know that he comes home at all odd hours, or maybe he has dropped in at the club for a bit.' He put his hand on her shoulder. 'Calm down, love. We'll have a bite, and then we wait, even if it takes all night.'

She shivered, as much from the cold as from emotional exhaustion. Uncle Sal pulled the folded sofa throw out from under her feet on the stool and wrapped it around her.

'I'll light the fire, and then I'll make us some sandwiches,' he said. 'Starving isn't going to help Rob.'

She nodded.

They ate in silence. Every sound was magnified in the stillness of the room, so that she could distinguish every crackling spark in the fireplace. The burning blue gum gave off a comforting smell.

Uncle Sal rekindled the fire for the second time when the sound of a car going onto the driveway to the back of the house set Frances's heart racing. She sat up straight, shaking all over.

Uncle Sal limped to the back door. 'Phil?'

'Give me ten minutes, okay?' came the muffled reply. These minutes lasted a lifetime.

Phil finally entered the sitting room, carrying two suitcases.

Frances's voice caught in her throat. 'You're not leaving, are you?'

He gave her a pitying look. 'I'm sorry, Franny, but I can't stay here, the way it is with your brother.' He sat down on an armchair. 'I'm really sorry.'

'The boy is innocent, Phil,' Uncle Sal said. A hint of steel gleamed in his eyes.

Phil said, 'Possible. I wouldn't know.' He raked his fingers through his brilliantined hair, making it stand on end. Grey shadows lined his eyes. 'This isn't easy for me either."

'You said you don't know if Rob's innocent," Frances said. Every word was an effort. 'Please, at least tell us what you do know. You owe us that much.'

Uncle Sal sat next to her, facing Phil with an unflinching stare. 'She's right, and it can't hurt you, can it?'

'Do we have a beer? Or something a bit stronger? I could do with a drink.'

Uncle Sal flung him the key to the sideboard. 'I got a bottle of whisky in there. Frances and I've still got our glasses.'

'Right-ho.' Phil got up and made a step towards Frances, before he turned around to get the whisky. He poured himself two inches high, gulped it down, and refilled his glass.

'Don't forget about us,' Uncle Sal said.

Phil filled their glasses as well, with a generous dose for Uncle Sal and a splash for Frances.

He sat down and stared at his drink. 'This morning, around 7.30, someone noticed that Adam Brockton, Brocky to his friends, hadn't turned up for work. A stable hand was sent out to rouse him and found him in his room. His head had been bashed in with a horseshoe, but he'd been dead already, killed with an overdose of horse tranquiliser and digitalin. He must have been asleep when the murderer injected the needle, rolled Brocky over and buried the syringe under his body.'

'That's why you arrested Rob.' Uncle Sal rubbed his chin. The first stubble poked through the skin, white and black interspersed, Frances noticed.

'But that's crazy,' she said. 'Why should my brother murder a blacksmith?'

'Have you ever heard about painted horses?' he said.

A faint memory stirred in her head. 'Didn't Jack mention them, Uncle Sal? But it's all a bit fuzzy.'

'It's a bit like a fake passport,' Uncle Sal said. 'You pass off an experienced horse with a good chance of winning as a novice, or another horse that usually crawls home long after the others have had their nose-bag. It's all about manipulating the odds, right?'

'That's it.'

'I understand that part,' Frances said, 'but I still don't see what that's got to do with Rob.'

'Franny, all the animals get a look-over from the vet. They may look pretty much all the same when you see them on the course, but up close? And then there's markings and such.' Phil paused.

'I'm sorry, Franny, but Alfie, the gelding that Brocky made a song about when you were at the races, had been painted. And he had presumably just won a race with big odds at the same racecourse where Rob and the blacksmith met.'

Uncle Sal rubbed his eyes. 'That doesn't look good.'

'No. Add to that the fact that Brocky was killed with things from Rob's bag, and that we found a betting slip for the race in case in his room that would have netted him fifty pounds, and it looks pretty conclusive.'

Frances shook her head. 'No. It's all a lie.'

Uncle Sal pulled her close. 'So, where are you going now, Phil?'

'The inspector found me a room in a boarding house.'

At least he had the grace to look embarrassed, Frances thought. 'So that's it. My brother's in trouble, and you're off.'

'What else do you expect me to do?'

'Stay.' Her voice trembled. 'Help us.'

'Hush, love.' Uncle Sal stroked her hand. 'We can't blame Phil for moving out. He can't very well lodge with the family of a potential murderer. It would make him look crooked, and us too.'

'I'm sorry, Frances,' Phil said again. 'I wish things were different, but they're not. All I can say is, I hope we'll meet again.' He made a curious pause. 'There's always the Top Note and Dolores. It's good to have a chat with old mates, eh, Uncle Sal.'

'Yes.' Uncle Sal blew out his breath. 'We'll catch up with you, no worries. One other thing, before you leave. Can you arrange for us to see the boy? And should we take him anything, clothes, shaving tackle?'

'I made sure we packed up his gear and sent it along after him. As for a visit, maybe I can fix something for the day after tomorrow. And, Frances?'

'Yes?'

'I gave the reporters his name as Theodore R Palmer, from Queensland, so that should give him some anonymity.' He smoothed down his unruly hair. 'Why doesn't he use his first name?'

'He hates it. When we were kids, one of our neighbours had a big slobbering bulldog named Teddy, and an elderly lady owned a poodle called Theo.' Frances blinked back tears. 'Can you imagine, one man constantly yelling, Teddy youse daftie, and the lady cooing, Theo lovie. It's been Rob ever since.'

'Yeah. I can see that.'

Phil got up and held out his hand, first to Frances who touched it briefly, then to Uncle Sal who shook it hard. 'No hard feelings? I'm only doing my job.'

'Sure,' Uncle Sal said. Frances nodded.

They both looked after Phil as he walked out of the house.

'You look all in, love,' Uncle Sal said after a long pause. 'What do you say, we turn in for tonight? Try to sleep, and tomorrow we'll talk to Jack and see what we three can cook up together.'

~

She must have dropped off as soon as her head touched the pillow, but her dreams were filled with faceless men, chasing her on horseback, with gigantic hypodermic needles in one hand.

Uncle Sal looked at her with concern as she dragged herself into the kitchen. He'd already prepared a pot of tea and buttered toast.

'You look fit to drop, love. Why don't you phone in sick and crawl back to bed? I'll bring you up a tray.'

'Thanks, Uncle Sal, but no. I'll be fine, and I need something to occupy my mind or I'll go crazy.' She took a slice of toast and forced herself to take a bite, and then another one, until she'd managed to eat it completely. Her stomach still felt a bit queasy but not too bad.

'Can you ring the police headquarter and found out where – where he is, and when we can see him? And ask them if he needs money, or food ...' The tears she'd held back since the moment she woke up, welled up in force. 'Oh, Uncle Sal, what are we going to do?'

'Easy enough,' he said, wiping her wet cheek with his handkerchief. 'Find out who's behind all this and bring the boy home. With your wits and mine and Jack's against our unknown villain, what could go wrong? And we've got our secret ally in Phil.'

'Do we? To me it sounded as if he couldn't wait to wash his hands of us.'

'Frances, he as good as said to come talk to him at the Top Note, where we can do so in privacy. Here.' He handed her his handkerchief and refilled their cups. 'I'll pick you up after work. If you need me sooner, just give me a bell, will you?'

Keeping her mind on her job was a constant struggle, but at least it gave her something to do, apart from fretting. She'd bought the newspaper on her way to work, from the sunken-cheeked man at the corner who had five children, a wife and elderly parents to support. And he was one of the luckier ones.

Every day there seemed to be more men and women roaming the streets, with worn-out clothes, hungry faces and dead eyes. Fifty pounds! You could live on that for months. No wonder the police believed without questioning that Rob would commit a crime to lay his hands on that much money.

The light bulbs on the switchboard flashed. Without thinking, she answered, plugged in the jacks to connect the call, and switched off again. At least Phil had been true to his word. The Advertiser had a lurid report about the horseshoe murder, as they called it, committed for the sake of greed. The heroic police had acted fast and held now in its cell a suspect, the cold-blooded veterinary surgeon, Theodore Palmer from Queensland.

A blurred photograph accompanied the article, of a man being pushed into a police vehicle. A burly officer half-covered his body, and the hat shaded his face. No-one would have recognised Rob from this picture.

The lights flashed again; back to duty.

Five minutes before her shift ended, Mr Gibbons crept into the room, trying hard to be as quiet as he could. Frances gave him a questioning glance as she finally got through to the operator in Dubbo. Long distance calls could be tricky. With so many switchboards involved it was like a relay race, relying on the baton not being dropped.

Her hand trembled as she took off the headset. 'Yes, Mr Gibbons? Is anything the matter?' Please, she prayed silently, let him not have made the connection with my brother from the story in the newspaper. Or the radio. She'd forgotten about the radio. What if they had mentioned Rob's full name? Sweat formed on her forehead.

'I wanted to thank you for the tickets,' he said. 'You've made me and my wife very happy.'

'I'm glad to hear that.'

'Oh yes, indeed.' He cleared his throat. 'There's one other thing though.'

Her heart missed a beat.

'When you asked for a few days off before the show, I said I'd look into it.'

'Yes?'

'I'm sorry to say I couldn't make it the whole time, but if it suits you, you could have your last shift in two days, and start again the Monday after the show. You've worked enough extra hours to cover most of that, so you'll only have to give up three days of annual leave.' He peered at her with concern. 'You do look as if you could with a bit of a rest. Don't work yourself too hard, my dear.'

'Thank you,' she said. 'It has been a busy few days, but I'll be fine.'

Clara opened the door. 'Hello Mr Gibbons. Off you go, Franny. Your Uncle Sal's already waiting for you.' A faint pink flushed her cheeks. 'He asked me save him a spot on my dance card. Doesn't he just have the loveliest manners?'

'Well, Clara, I reckon I'd better ask you for a dance too before you're all booked up," Mr Gibbons said, with a twinkle in his eyes.

'Ooh.' Clara's eyes widened with delight. Good on her.

'Bye.' Frances slipped out of the room.

Uncle Sal enveloped her in his arm. 'How are you holding up, love?'

She swallowed. 'Good enough. Have you –have you heard anything?'

He looked around with a meaningful glance. People bustled about, with hawkers announcing their clothes pegs, shoelaces and potholders in increasingly desperate voices, while errand boys hopped it to and from offices, shops and the post office. 'We'll talk at home.'

'What is it?' she said as soon as they'd walked through the front door. 'Please, Uncle Sal. I need to know.'

She followed him through to the kitchen. He lit the wood-burning stove and put the kettle on before he lowered himself onto a chair. 'We can see him tomorrow afternoon but only for ten minutes. The officer I spoke to said Rob's keeping up well and only talks about the horse he treated. He worries about the animal.'

'He would.' Frances struggled to keep back tears. 'Does he need anything? What are we allowed to bring?'

'They didn't say, but I reckon a few quid won't go amiss, and maybe a book or two to read.' He bent down to massage his ankle. 'I only wish they'd let me see him for a quick geek. Mind you, the place looked clean enough, and they're not holding too many folks there, so it didn't seem too bad.'

Images from the pictures flashed in her mind. Rob was in a cell, and cells were bug-infested places, full of stomach-turning odours. And they held dangerous people.

'Does he – does he have to share a cell?'

'I don't think so,' Uncle Sal said. 'Like I said, they're not doing too much business. We'll see for ourselves tomorrow. But now we'll have our tea, and then we'll wait for Jack to ring up. I've got something important to ask him.'

'Which is?'

'If he knows of a good lawyer who specialises in criminal cases. Phil said we'd better make sure we get the best man on Rob's case. Murder carries the death penalty.'

# CHAPTER SIX

'*J*'ll come home on the next boat,' Jack said, as soon as Frances mentioned Rob's plight. For once she didn't care if the operator was listening in. This was too important to bother about small things.

How typical of Jack not to ask any questions but to come straight to her rescue.

If only it were so easy. She pointed out, 'You only arrived in New Zealand. Your sister needs you.'

'As do you. Rachel will understand.'

Frances closed her eyes, picturing the concerned gleam in his eyes. 'There must be something I can do or ask him. Uncle Sal and I are allowed a short visit in an hour.'

'I'll send Bluey to do a little bit of questioning around the racecourses,' Jack said. 'If this blacksmith identified the horse, odds are they pulled that stunt on other courses too. And you ask your brother exactly when and why he was hired.'

'You think he was used as a patsy?' Frances had asked herself that question over and over again.

'Sounds reasonable. He's young, he needs money, and he's new to the races. It would take a memorable attribute for him to remember a horse he's given a quick once-over a few weeks or months ago,' Jack said.

'You're right.'

The operator said, 'Your three minutes are up.'

'I'll ring up tomorrow,' Jack said.

The phone went silent.

Frances borrowed some of her mother's church-going clothes for the visit and scraped back her hair in a severe bun. Uncle Sal wore his most somber outfit too.

Frances tried to not dwell on the fact that the last occasion on which he'd worn the charcoal suit had been a funeral. He looked almost like a stranger, without the accustomed gleam in his eyes and his stage-honed presence.

They'd practiced their arrival at the prison. So much might hang for Rob on their looking trustworthy, and respectable.

They'd wrapped a cake and a few sausages from the German butcher in brown paper, to make it easy for the guards to check. Uncle Sal carried the foodstuff well away from the toiletries and clothes Frances took along for Rob.

The ruddy-faced guard only gave them and their parcels a cursory glance. A young woman and a lame old man didn't seem to pose much of a threat for him, Frances thought as she gave him her sweetest smile.

She tried to hide her shock as she saw Rob. How could he look this gaunt already? His skin stretched over his cheekbones, and underneath his tan was an unhealthy pallor.

'You shouldn't have come,' he said. 'This is not a place for you, Franny.'

He hadn't called her Franny since they were little. She blinked away the sudden moistness in her eyes. 'Nonsense,' she said. 'As if I would stay away.'

She reached out for him, separated only by a few inches. The guard had taken them to a small visiting room, with bolted-down chairs and a table that was also fastened to the floor.

'How are they treating you?' Uncle Sal asked, his voice, that could easily fill a music hall, carefully lowered.

'Fair enough.' Rob rubbed his temples. 'But I can't find out about the bay horse I was treating. If the stable lad made a mistake, or I gave the wrong orders ...'

He slumped in his chair.

'We'll find out,' Frances said. 'But first you need to tell us a few things.' She glanced around, unsure if they were overheard and how long they would have.

'I don't know anything.'

Frances checked her list. 'Who hired you? And did you see that painted horse before?'

'I don't think so. But it's not impossible. All we do is a quick health check. I couldn't be fooled when it comes to passing off a five-year old racer as a two-year old, but apart from that, there is no reason to remember every horse unless it's got distinctive features." Rob's jaw worked. 'Poor old Brocky would check the hooves.'

'And you were inexperienced as a racecourse vet,' Uncle Sal said. 'Another point that would've made it easier to fool you. Who's your boss?'

'Technically, a group of racecourse managers. At least that's what I've been told. My pay envelope was handed over by Mr Lucca.'

'Mr Lucca?' Frances scribbled down that name.

'He's the assistant of Mr Dunne, the manager for Morphettville,' Rob said.

'Who would have access to your room, and to Brocky's lodgings?'

'We didn't always lock them,' Rob said. 'At least I didn't. My wallet was in my coat, and I had nothing else to steal.'

'What about your bag?'

'I always keep that with me.'

Frances bit her lip. No wonder Rob was the only suspect.

'Where was it exactly when you were treating the colicky horse?' Uncle Sal gave Frances's knee a tiny pat.

'I put it by the door,' Rob said. 'I didn't want the horse to roll over it, or myself to stumble. Within easy reach and yet out of the way.'

'And you were alone?'

'Only for a few minutes, while I sent the boy to fetch hot water and towels.'

'But you would have noticed anyone else entering?' Frances's heart beat a painful staccato in her chest. This was the important question. There was no reason to steal from Rob's bag, or to plant the betting slip, before Brocky had cried foul play and needed to be silenced.

'No idea. Lucy always says a whole travelling circus could pass through behind my back and I wouldn't hear them when I'm busy.'

His voice cracked as he mentioned his wife.

Frances reached out for Rob's arm. 'She's fine. She knows you wouldn't do anything crooked. Ever.'

A loud bang at the door interrupted them. 'Time's up.'

'Is there anything you need?' Uncle Sal asked.

Rob shook his head.

'We'll be back,' Frances said. 'Don't forget to eat and to take care of yourself. Promise?'

Rob nodded. 'Right-oh.'

It broke Frances's heart to leave her brother behind. He'd tried to say calm, but she could tell he didn't hold out much hope. They had to get him out of there, and fast, before prison crushed his spirits. She didn't dare consider failure. Not when Rob's life was at stake.

# CHAPTER SEVEN

*M*r Dunne and Mr Lucca. Frances circled the names in ink. They needed a list of everyone who worked at Morphettville, or had worked there, and knew his way around stables and lodgings at night. Surely there were security guards too, making their regular rounds.

Frances buried her head in her hands. Uncle Sal handed her a steaming mug of tea and dropped two lumps of sugar in it. It was almost too sweet, but she drank it gratefully.

'We've made some impressive progress,' he said, to cheer her up.

'Do you think so?'

'I sure do.' Uncle Sal counted on his fingers. 'We know our murderer was involved in racing at the racecourse where the blacksmith worked before. Remember it was only a fluke Brocky ended up in

Adelaide, instead of sticking to close to home as he usually did.'

'That's true.' A feeling of warmth spread through Frances's body. 'If we can find out on which racecourses Brocky worked, and who else worked there, we could narrow our list of suspects down.'

'We also need a list of the bookies.'

Frances frowned. 'Why?' While betting was a popular pastime, the bookies were still hoping they could set up shop on the racecourses, especially one like prestigious Morphettville, that had been honoured by a visit from the Prince of Wales in 1920 during his empire tour.

'I do have a few friends left your mother wouldn't have approved of.' Uncle Sal twinkled at her. 'And there's always Captain Jack's network. You've seen for yourself how close the veterans are.'

She broke into her first real smile since Rob's arrest. 'He and Bluey must have friends all over the country.' Jack's military title, dating back to the Great Stoush, still opened doors due to the fact that he looked after his men even long after their return. Most of the staff at the Top Note had served under him, and he felt that obligation keenly. One of the first things he'd done after shifting to Adelaide was holding a charity ball for war veterans and nurses. Frances half-wished she'd been there. Her more sensible part realised it was better like this. At Christmas 1928 she'd been only nineteen, and

Jack had taken long enough to ignore the difference in their age.

Uncle Sal rose and opened the icebox they'd purchased last month. Frances had reasoned it would pay for itself, with the savings in food that normally would have spoilt in the Adelaide heat. Now she regretted the expense. Rob needed a lawyer, and he'd have one, if she had to beg for a second mortgage on their home.

'We have a left-over pie,' he said. 'Or I can fry lamb chops. You need a proper meal inside you.'

'Pie is fine,' she said. If only Phil could yell them if there were any news, or a clue to the real murderer. Instead, he'd left them, and Jack was on the other side of the Tasman Sea.

'At least I only have to make it through tomorrow at work,' she said. 'I wish I didn't have to go.'

'You could snoop around,' Uncle Sal said as he slid the pie in a frying-pan and covered it with a lid. He'd learnt all kinds of tricks and shortcuts as a Vaudeville artist.

'But how?'

'Chat with the other operators, if you can. See if there were other rumours about something funny at the races in the cities.'

'That's a good idea.' It should be easy enough. All the operators overheard stuff without the people on the phone thinking about it. While it was strictly forbidden to talk about it, most of the girls knew they could chat freely among themselves. Frances preferred to stick to the rules, but not when bending them could help her brother.

She gave Uncle Sal a peck on the cheek. 'You're the best.'

He patted her back with his left hand while he flipped the pie. 'You and I, eh?'

'You and I.'

Halfway through her shift, Frances could have screamed with disappointment. Whenever she tried to bring up the racecourse murder with a colleague in another city, they would be cut short by a new call. Where were the quiet days when so few people would spend precious money on telephone calls that Mr Gibbons had to lay off half the staff? Today it seemed like all of Australia waited in line to talk to Adelaide.

Four hours later, and the only morsel she had was that one girl's brother's father-in-law, who used to end up with empty pockets, came home about a month ago from a race in Flemington flush with money.

'Are you crook?' Gussie asked as Frances took off her headset. 'Your face is all red.'

'Just a bit of a headache. I'm glad I'll have a bit of a break.'

'I can't wait to see the show.' Gussie's face held a dreamy look. 'My mum says it'll be ever so posh.'

'Not too posh for the likes of us, but yeah, it will be special.' Frances forced her muscles into a smile. The idea of the Top Note without Jack, while Rob sat in a cell, was unbearable, but there was nothing to be done about it.

She waved good-bye and stepped out into the street when a hand clasped her shoulder from behind.

Frances stifled a shriek and spun around, ready to use her handbag as a weapon, when she recognized Bluey.

'Sorry,' he said, with a contrite look on his broad face. 'I didn't mean to startle you.'

'What is it?' she asked. 'It's not about Jack, is it?' What if he'd met with an accident, or maybe he couldn't leave his sister. She fumbled for her handkerchief.

'Marie said to fetch you in the car. Uncle Sal's already waiting.' Bluey took her by the arm.

'That's very thoughtful,' she said. 'Bless her.' Bluey's wife would help her. Marie Fitzpatrick was just as reliable and trustworthy as her husband and tackled any problem head-on. As a former nurse on a veterans' ward she too had connections everywhere.

Frances sank back into the upholstered seat. Her head whirled. Maybe Dolores could wheedle some information out of Phil. After all, it wouldn't hurt anyone to let them know where the blacksmith's trail led.

Uncle Sal sat centre-stage, twirling on a wheeled chair. Frances's best friend Pauline gave him a push whenever he slowed down until he held up his hand. 'Not too fast,' he said, miming throwing a knife. 'We need to time this just right.'

Frances clapped. Pauline squeaked as she spun around and almost lost her balance. Frances hadn't seen the roller skates before, but she was glad her idea seemed to work out. At least something did.

'Wasn't that spiffing?' Pauline asked, her dimples growing deeper every second.

'Marvellous,' Frances agreed. She gave Uncle Sal a questioning look. He shook his head the fraction of an inch. He hadn't told Pauline. The fewer people knew about Rob, the safer was his secret for now.

'I could do with a break,' Uncle Sal said. 'Thank you, Pauline, and give my love to Dolores. I'm sure she wants you back.'

'Not for ages.' Pauline pulled a face. 'She's got a dress-fitting, and she won't let anybody see the gown until it's perfect.' A grin flitted over her face. 'But Tony should be upstairs. He's fixing something in Mr Jack's apartment.' She winked at Frances. 'I hope you'll like whatever he's doing.'

She pushed herself off Uncle Sal's chair and rolled across the floor.

Uncle Sal hopped up, his chair still in motion.

'Careful,' Frances said.

Marie peeked through the door and motioned them

over. "Tucker's ready." She'd put out sandwiches with slabs of ham, and the orange pound cake Uncle Sal was partial too, in the office. 'I thought you'd like some privacy,' Marie said. 'It's a bit cramped, but better than having any joker earwig on what's going on.'

Tears prickled in Frances's eyes. She really needed to get a grip on her emotions. 'Thank you.'

'No worries.' Marie opened the door as soon as she heard footfall in the hallway. Bluey, with a couple of wooden chairs.

Uncle Sal wolfed down a sandwich. 'I reckon Jack has told you all about our little spot of bother.'

Marie nodded. 'We'll make sure it stays between us.'

'What do you think?' Frances asked.

'Same as you. Somebody left your brother holding the bag.' Bluey helped himself to a slice of cake, using a napkin as a plate. He ate leaning against the wall, although they had one free chair left.

'What I don't understand is, why kill the blacksmith?' Uncle Sal eyed the cake. He wasn't a particularly vain man, but Frances understood his need to cut a dapper figure on stage, especially if he had to perform seated. She handed him a slab and took one herself.

'How big would the penalty be for sending a painted horse into a race? It can't be that much if you compare it to the big drop.'

The cake stuck in Frances's throat. Death sentences were rare, but the existence of the gallows inside Adelaide's prison was a stark reminder of the fate that awaited a convicted murderer. Less than two years ago, a man called Thomas Blyth had been hanged for the murder of his wife.

The door opened again while Uncle Sal's words still hung in the air.

'Only one reason,' a male voice said. 'It must have been about a lot more than just one horse, and they must have felt secure they had stitched up Rob good.'

Frances squeezed her cake so tight it crumbled into the floor as she turned her head. 'Jack? But that's not possible.'

But there he stood, solid and comforting and with that lazy smile that promised everything would be alright. He pressed a kiss onto her forehead and took a sandwich. 'I haven't had a bite since this morning,' he said.

'But the boat takes days.' Frances couldn't shake her confusion. 'You were in New Zealand only yesterday.'

'I was there until dawn this morning. An old mate owns a flight service, going back and forth, and he took me over in his Fokker.' Jack sat down and stretched his legs.

'You were flying?'

'I tried to talk him out of it,' Marie said. 'But he didn't listen.'

'A plane that's good enough for Charles Kingsford Smith, is good enough for me.'

'They all say that until they crash.' Marie glared at him.

'Would you have said that if Bluey were in prison?' Jack's voice held an edge of finality even Marie accepted without another word. 'Now I'm here, what do we have to go on with?'

'One of the girls in Melbourne told me about an unexpected win in Flemington. That's all,' Frances said, aware of how little that told them.

'That's a good start.' Jack stroked her cheek. 'Nobody would be crazy enough to have a painted horse start in one of the big races like the Melbourne Cup, but the race days around it would bring in a fair number of punters. Bluey, you find us someone in each city who either likes a flutter and would have paid attention to unexpectedly high wins for rank outsiders, or a bookie. A straight one, we can trust.'

'I can ask around too. Lots of show people like a bit of fun when they travel around,' Uncle Sal said. 'The races are just what they're looking for.'

'Good-oh.' Bluey took a notepad from the desk and a pencil. 'If I have names, maybe Miss Frances can get their phone numbers quicker than me, if they are on the phone.'

'Leave it to me,' Frances said, relieved to finally have something concrete to do. Trust Jack to lift her spirits. Although he had taken a huge risk, flying across the thousands of miles of open water between New Zealand and Australia. Too many planes never made it safely even on small distances, over land.

'Frances?' Jack's voice snapped her back to the present situation. 'We'll sort this. You'll have your brother back.'

# CHAPTER EIGHT

*J*ack sent Uncle Sal and Frances home with Bluey. He'd tried to keep up a cheerful face in front of them, but Rob Palmer really was in one hell of a mess. That's why he had dropped everything, kissed his sister good-bye and entrusted his life to a machine made out of thin metal and death rattles. The sooner they figured out what was going on at the races, the better, before all possible suspects had moved on and the trail was not only cold, but obliterated.

He knocked on Dolores' apartment door.

'Come in,' she sang out.

He entered, only to have her look scared at the first. 'I didn't expect you for ages,' she said. She pulled him towards the settee in front of her fireplace. The silk of her dress rustled gently. 'Why are you here? Is it about Rachel?'

'She's fine, and she sends you her love.'

'And her bloke? Did you suss him out?' Dolores creased her brows for a moment before she remembered to smooth out the lines on her expertly made-up face.

She took her beauty seriously, secretly convinced that half her admirers would stop listening to her sing if her looks were gone. She was wrong, Jack thought, but her bouts of insecurity were as much part of her as her indisputable talent, and her kindness.

'You'd like him,' he said. 'Strong enough to carry two sheep under his arms and the sort of man who'd actually do that if they needed help.'

'Good.' She held up her cocktail shaker, a question in her eyes. 'Martini?'

'If you have enough. I assume you're expecting Phil?'

'He said he might drop in.' A faint blush spread over her throat. It must be getting serious for her, then. Dolores, who'd been widowed just before the end of the war, hadn't had a serious relationship since she met Phil Anderson, an old war mate of Jack's, and, more importantly, her dead husband's.

The only stumbling block between them was the fact that Phil worked for the police and Dolores sang in a night club that served alcohol after booze became illegal every evening at the stroke of six o'clock. They seemed to have found their way around that issue, but Jack didn't want to bet on it.

Dolores poured the drinks. They clinked glasses as a rap on the door interrupted them.

Dolores rushed to the door only to slow down at the last moment. She opened and leant against the frame. 'Hello, darling,' she said.

Phil clasped her shoulders and kissed her with passion. 'I've missed you.'

'Hi, Phil,' Jack said, before the situation became embarrassing for anyone.

Phil shook his hand. 'I should've known you'd come to Frances's rescue.'

'Somebody had to.'

Dolores slipped away, giving them privacy.

'Who do you think did it?' Jack asked.

'If it wasn't Rob, I don't know.'

'You can't suspect him.'

Phil smoothed back his hair. 'As a policeman, I can't afford not to. It's not about my emotions, just the facts.'

'Good to hear. That's what I'm after.'

'In what way?'

'I need a list of the racecourse where the victim shooed the horses.'

Phil blew out his breath. 'That's a tall order. I don't think we would have looked to deeply. Not with a suspect in the cells.'

'But you can do it.'

'I'll try. That's the best I can say.'

'I'll take that. Also, jockeys.'

Phil gave him a blank stare.

'If anyone would remember a horse, it should be the jockey, right? Gait, colouring, mannerism, I'll take anything. And they'd know their way around the stables and lodgings without anyone paying them attention.'

'Fair point. But I'd have to have my superior's permission, and he thinks Rob's a dead cert for the murder.' Phil motioned towards Jack's cocktail. 'Any of that left?'

'Help yourself.'

Phil sipped in silence. 'Excellent drink.'

'Dolores made it. And the sooner you tell me all you can, the sooner she can come out of her bedroom and entertain you.'

That spurred Phil on. 'You want the racing programmes. I don't know if there's an archive, but they shouldn't be too hard to get hold off.' Phil's gaze flickered towards the bedroom door.

'I'll call in at the club tomorrow night with any information I have.'

'Good-oh.' Jack rose. 'I appreciate that.'

'Well, if the kid's innocent, I'm only doing my job. If he's guilty, I'm not doing any harm.' Phil led Jack to the door and shook his hand again. 'It's good to have you back. Dolores was wearing a path in the carpet, but don't tell her I said that.'

Jack and Bluey's network sprang into action overnight. They might be separated by thousands of miles, but the years in the trenches forged bonds they'd never forget. A summons from Captain Jack should be good enough to guarantee the spreading of information from coast to coast.

They'd converted part of Jack's office into a campaign headquarters. Marie had organised a huge map of Australia with pins marking bigger racecourses. Jack had decided they could ignore the small ones. Fraud was too risky to engage in for a handful of pennies. Everywhere they could be sure of a contact in place was marked with a note of the name pinned next to it. A list with more names sat on the desk, waiting to be handed over to Frances for research.

Jack estimated if they reached ten men, or women thanks to Marie's contacts, within 48 hours that number should easily quadruple. He didn't fear any gossip reaching the wrong ears. A request from one veteran to another would assure no questions being asked.

He yawned as he surveyed the map. Two men in Sydney and one each in Melbourne and Perth had already been contacted and promised to report back by nightfall.

'Did you sleep at all? You look all in.' Marie propelled him towards his chair.

'Not a lot. First too much yacking with the family, and then, well, you know.' He yawned again, prompting Marie to fetch a fresh pot of coffee. 'Hot as hell and black as a mine pit,' she said.

He gulped it down, waiting for the energy surge to kick in. 'How are the rehearsals going?' he asked.

'Uncle Sal's act is going to be beaut,' she said. 'That is, if Frances doesn't pull out. I wish I could step in, but Bluey almost blew his top.'

'Fancy that. Not too keen to have someone throw knives at you, while he's running after the littlees?'

Marie pouted. 'I don't see what he's fussing about. You're not clucking over Frances like a broody mother hen.'

Laughter rose in Jack's throat, the first genuine laugh since he'd heard about Rob. 'I leave that to Uncle Sal. And the rest?'

'Will be just as you want it. We could have five times as many orchestras and sell at least twice as many seats.' She sighed. 'As much as I love the talkies, it's a shame we don't have the music anymore.'

'True,' he said. 'Do we have any tickets left?'

'Maybe a dozen. Why?'

'Just a thought. Where's Bluey?'

'Yacking away with a cove at the garage, who used to drive horse floats to Morphettville.' A sly grin spread over Marie's face. 'He's taken the Rover to have the engine checked. His idea.'

'I assume that'll take a few hours.'

'I can easily take over phone duty,' Marie said. 'Dolores is dead-set on showing you her new number, but she promised not to bother you.'

'Who did she promise?'

'Herself.' Marie nudged him aside and sat down at his desk. 'I'll call you if anything happens.'

Jack strolled towards the main room, so deep in thought he almost collided with a tuba player on his way to rehearsal.

'Sorry,' the man said. 'She's a bit unwieldy.' He patted his instrument case.

'No worries. How are things shaping up?'

'Bonzer, Mr Sullivan.' The man beamed. His clothes were at least one size too big but fitted too well when it came to length to have been hand-me-downs.

'And the food and all the rest?' Some men could be prickly when it came to accepting charity. Going hungry meant nothing to them compared to being considered a bludger, and with an unemployment rate close to thirty percent, having an empty belly wasn't even considered a hardship.

Jack found himself whistling a tune he'd heard only too often lately. Children sang it like a kind of nursery rhyme.

The tuba player gave him a resigned shrug as he sang softly, 'We're on the susso now, we can't afford a cow. We live in a tent, we pay no rent, we're on the susso now.' He stopped. 'I'd be on the susso now if it weren't for you.'

Jack winced. The food-dole, as South Australia knew it, or susso was only available if people had been unemployed for a long enough period. Only then they'd be able to receive food vouchers for meagre enough rations.

The employment Jack could offer the musicians covered a few weeks, which would then count against them when they applied for government help. All he could do was offer them decent pay, and decent meals. Marie sent the men home with food parcels, so their families could eat, but they couldn't feed all of Adelaide.

With the whole world starving, he could understand why people might be tempted to cheat on the racecourse. Murder though, and framing an innocent man, was in a different league.

The tuba player peered at him. 'Did I say anything wrong?'

Jack clapped him on the back. 'Just wool-gathering. Dolores happy?'

'She's the best singer I've ever met,' the musician said. 'Doesn't need many cues and always has a smile for everyone. Not that she'd look at anyone but her fella.'

'Good to hear,' Jack said. 'But I mustn't keep you.' He held the door open for the tuba player and followed him.

On the stage, the orchestra was setting up. A small area was curtained off, as a private place for Dolores where she would warm her vocal cords or sit down for a spell. On another part of the stage, the silhouette drawn onto a door had been replaced by a seven feet tall wooden circle, with metal straps to hold Frances's hands and feet in place. The circle wouldn't spin, but even this should be enough for the thrill seekers.

Jack wiped his brow with a handkerchief. They day

was hot already, and soon the huge ceiling fans would blast.

Dolores didn't like them on when she rehearsed, although the whirr should be faint enough to be inaudible over the music.

High heels clacked on the floor in a rhythm he'd recognise anywhere. He slowly turned around, to see Frances's worried face before him. Uncle Sal too appeared drawn and tired. For the first time since he met him, the entertainer showed every year of his age.

'Do you have any news?' Frances asked.

'Soon.'

The orchestra picked up its first tune, one unfamiliar to Jack. That must be the number Dolores had fallen in love with.

Uncle Sal tapped his feet.

'We should watch her,' Jack said. 'Then we can talk.'

Frances did her best to hide her disappointment, but gave in. 'Sure,' she said.

They sat down on some of the chairs at the back of the room.

Dolores swept onto the stage, a spotlight trained on the microphone and her face. Her dark eyes lit up as she saw Jack and she started to sing, 'Dream A Little Dream Of Me'.

Frances swayed in rhythm with the music.

Jack made a mental note to purchase a recording of the song for his apartment. His supplier had a standing order to deliver all the latest music from the United

States and Great Britain to Dolores, but Jack rarely bought them for himself. If he felt like listening to someone apart from Dolores, he could always knock on her door. That is, until lately. He'd arranged for a discreet signal when Dolores had a visitor. Since Phil's arrival, the potted cactus on a two-tiered shelf next to her door sat on the lower shelf at least twice a week.

# CHAPTER NINE

*I*n Ballarat, veteran Arthur Dowling sniffed the pungent air. Horse sweat and jacaranda, mixed with fresh hay and baked soil might not be to everyone's liking. For Arthur, they smelt sweeter than his old lady's perfume.

He lingered in the entrance to the boxes where he'd find his mate Curly. Nobody remembered his real name, thanks to his almost complete baldness as soon as he hit twenty. Curly had been a jockey when the war broke out. He'd planned on enlisting like the rest of them, when he took a tumble that broke his shoulder in enough places to leave him with a slightly stiff arm. Ever since, he'd worked as a stable lad for the Ballarat Turf Club.

The rhythmic scrape of a horse brush told Art which box Curly worked in. He rapped softly on the wooden door, careful not to alarm the beautiful bay mare. She seemed calm enough, but one never could be sure with turf horses. Some lived on nerves and speed. Others were as placid as work horses.

Arthur had worked alongside Curly once, for three glorious years. Nowadays he counted himself lucky to deliver groceries for a store twice a week.

'Hiya, mate,' he said. 'That's a real beauty you're having there.'

Curly twisted his neck without interrupting the brushing. 'Art. What brings you here?'

'I haven't seen you for a while, and I kind of missed being around the horses. You know how it is.' With the stable lad having been forced to spend the war at home, Arthur had no intention to bring up Bluey or Captain Jack.

He held out his hand for the horse. She moved closer and rubbed her soft nose in his skin. 'Is she racing?'

'Why? You planning on having a flutter on the fillies?' The mare neighed. Curly patted her neck. 'Although this one is a proper racer.'

'I would if I could be sure it's all a fair go.' Arthur shrugged. 'Gets you thinking, this business in Adelaide.'

'Too right it does.' Curly put away the brush and replaced it with a hoof scraper. He lifted one hoof up on his knee, his stiff shoulder for one moment causing him to wince.

'Can you imagine waltzing out of one arvo's racing with your pockets full of cash?'

'That'd be the day.'

'Yeah. Not likely, is it.' Arthur paused, to give Curly a pause for thought. It worked, because Curly said, 'Mind you, there was this one race, on cup week, when that little brown mare came flying out of nowhere on the last few furlongs and left all the favourites in the dust. Odds of 85 to two, she paid.' Curly had finished with the first hoof and lifted the second one.

'Cup week, eh?' That made sense, Arthur thought. Although Ballarat was more than one hundred miles away from Melbourne, the Ballarat Cup attracted every man and his dog. 'Remember her name? In case she's running when I'm off to see my brother in Geelong.'

'Something boring, they'd called her. Lady Lilly or something like that. Not like his one.' He set down the hoof.

Arthur peered on the blackboard at the side of the box. 'Mistral. Sounds nice.'

'Yeah. It does.'

'Which reminds me. My brother is mad keen on old racing programmes. Reads them like the bible. You wouldn't be able to put your mitts on some?'

'That shouldn't be too hard.' Curly gave him a sly glance. 'I could bring some along to the pub tonight.'

'Cheers, mate. Beer's on me.'

Arthur hurried to the post office. He had to be careful with his pennies, but Bluey had promised that Captain Jack would see them right, and he never broke a promise. If he had played his hand right with Curly, he'd also be able to send the material they were needing in Adelaide. That, together with the titbit about Lady Lilly, would go a long ways to pay back Captain Jack for saving Arthur's life in January 1918, when he'd brought him down just as Arthur was going to leave the trench. He'd landed flat on his face, breathing in stinking mud, while bullets soared overhead.

Marie whistled through her teeth as she typed out the notes from the three phone calls she'd received. That done, she slipped two pound-notes each in an envelope, addressed to her callers via their local post offices. She didn't dare leave her post, so instead she'd entrust her oldest daughter, who dropped in after school for a chat and afternoon tea before going home, with posting them. Sophie loved the Top Note as much as her parents did, and if Marie had allowed it, all the staff would have spoilt her rotten. The post office was only a few minutes away, and everyone in the neighbourhood knew Sophie. She'd be safe with the money.

When Sophie popped in, Marie put her typed notes away. Her daughter was the most level-headed nine-year old imaginable, but there was no need for her to know anything about fraud and murder and the fact that her parents had any part in playing sleuths. Sophie's favourite book was the Hardy Boys' mystery Captain Jack had given her for her birthday, but at her age, the excitement should be limited to fiction.

'No cake today?' Sophie fluttered her eyelashes at her mother as she placed her school bag in the corner. Her big blue eyes looked so much like her father's that Marie had to smile.

'There should be an apple crumble in the kitchen, all waiting for us. Can you please fetch it? And see if Daddy's back?'

'Right-oh.' Sophie skipped through the door. Marie thought of Frances's brother and his family. How terrified they must be. She could only hope and pray the answer to their troubles could be found in the information they were collecting.

An hour later, Sophie was on her way home, and they held their first proper meeting. Frances held up well, Marie thought, considering the circumstances. She'd used powder to cover the dark smudges under her eyes, but she was calm and composed as she sat framed by Uncle Sal and Captain Jack.

Bluey stood beside the map, pins at the ready.

'We've heard back from Ballarat, Yarra Glen and Fremantle,' Marie said. 'The stories all sound the same.

Unknown horses, with long odds and total winnings of a few thousand pounds each time.'

'Since when?' Jack asked.

'Since the Easter races last year at the least.'

'So, my contact in Melbourne was right,' Frances said. 'Something weird is going on at the racecourses.'

'I guess they thought their old vet would become suspicious. That's why they hired your brother instead. The blacksmith only came to Morphettville as a last-minute substitute.' Jack flicked through Marie's notes. 'Yarra Glen is where he met your brother, and where he says the painted horse ran. Only it wasn't called Alfie back then.'

'Who could pull off this kind of fraud?' Uncle Sal asked. 'The trainer? The owner? The jockey?'

Bluey cleared his throat.

Jack give his right-hand man an encouraging nod.

'From what I've learned, it depends,' he said. 'A trainer would see what filly has potential, but unless he travels along, there's no way of telling if someone switched papers when they list them.'

'Wouldn't they see in which races the horse ran?' Frances sat up a little straighter, Jack noticed with satisfaction. She'd always be a fighter,

'Yes and no. My mate says it's not too hard to say, the horse was off its feed or something and had to be scratched. The same goes for the owner. And the jockeys are lucky if they ride the same horse in more than a few races.' Bluey gave Jack an apologetic look.

'Which means it all comes down to Morphettville. Whoever needed the blacksmith silenced, would either have been there in person, or phoned up someone who'd kill on his order.' Jack took Frances's hand and gave it a gentle squeeze. 'Is it possible for you to find out if there were any phone calls made to Morphettville after Brocky's accusation?'

Frances hung her head. 'Not likely. There are no logs, and we are all sworn to discretion.'

'I feared as much,' Jack said. 'Which means, there are no easy ways to narrow down our suspects.'

'Is there anything we can do at all?' Frances's voice held a slight quiver.

'Sure. Marie and Bluey will comb through the racing programmes as soon as they arrive and make a list of all names with a connection to Morphettville.'

A rap on the door interrupted Jack. 'Come in,' he said.

Phil's voice answered. 'Can you come outside for a minute?'

Jack stepped into the passage. The two men gazed at each other in silence.

'I'm not really here,' Phil said.

'I thought so.'

Phil blew out his breath in frustration. 'Listen, mate, I really tried, but for us the case is closed. We have no interest to look into any goings-on at Morphettville.'

'No names then.'

'Sorry. The best I could come up with is a few names

of the jokers who hired and paid the blacksmith. He kept an account we found in his swag.' Phil slipped a piece of paper into Jack's hand.

'Thanks. I appreciate that.' Jack hesitated. 'You've heard there were a few races in Victoria where a rank outsider made some lucky punters very happy?'

'Where? Melbourne?'

'Fremantle racecourse. You still have contacts among your old colleagues, I assume.'

'And young Palmer was up in Queensland with his arm up a sheep's bottom until lately.' For an instant, a light flashed in Phil's eyes before he sighed. 'Not much use, is it? Sorry I can't be of any more help.'

Jack clapped him on the back. 'Go and see Dolores. She'll be waiting already.'

As soon as he opened the office door, four heads swiveled towards him. 'I want to help with the names,' Frances said.

'You'll be too busy for that,' Jack said. 'As will Salvatore the Magnificent.'

Uncle Sal chortled. 'You've got a plan.'

'I do. If you're willing to take a slight risk.'

'I don't care what I have to do if it's for Rob.' Frances attempted a smile.

'Good. Because if we can't get the names we need from anyone else, they will keep a log at the racecourse.'

'But how?' Uncle Sal looked puzzled.

'We'll take our show to Morphettville. Do you know

how to pick locks, Uncle Sal?' Jack's grin held a dangerous edge.

Uncle Sal wiggled his fingers. 'I'm a bit rusty but give me a couple of days and I'll be able to break into Bank of England.'

# CHAPTER TEN

rances waited until she and Uncle Sal were back home, before she confronted him. 'You can't be serious.'

'I don't know what you mean.'

'Picking locks!'

'It's not hard. Anyone who helped with magic tricks used to be able to do it.' Uncle Sal huffed a little. 'A little bit of refreshing, that's all I need. I used to be a wiz with my hands. Houdini himself said so when we met in Europe long before you were born.'

Frances hugged him as tight as she could. She shivered despite the warmth of the evening. The house, usually so comforting with its familiar smells and looks, had an air of desolation made worse by the pictures of Rob and his family on the mantel.

'I don't doubt your skills,' Frances said. 'But I'm scared about what would happen if you get caught.'

'You worry too much,' Uncle Sal said. 'I'm sure Jack will have a plan for anything.'

Frances relented. 'Are you sure?'

Uncle Sal crossed is heart.

'In that case, can you teach me?'

He gaped at her. 'Teach you what?'

'Lock picking. I'm your assistant, remember?'

Uncle Sal opened his mouth and shut it again.

'You said it yourself, Jack will take care of us.'

Jack needed all his persuasion to convince Marie to leave. He sent Bluey home as well. There would be enough long days again soon, and the rest of the staff could function without them on a normal night.

Jack peered over the balustrade on the upper floor. The crowd seemed happy and well-behaved enough, Dolores new songs were received with enough applause to quieten her flashes of self-doubt, and as he'd hoped, half a dozen luminaries including two councillors and a judge were among the guests. The Top Note attracted the upper echelons of Adelaide society thanks to its amenities and the fact that the only law broken here was the one regarding the six pm alcohol ban.

Jack had worked hard for his reputation. Would he really be willing to pay the price if he and everyone he cared about as caught up in a hare-brained scheme to solve a murder?

He gripped the balustrade tight enough for his knuckles to turn white. Stepping aside and doing nothing was impossible. Risking everything he'd built and what it meant for the people who depended upon him was likewise not an option. He needed a plan, not just the blithe declaration he'd given Frances.

'Captain Jack?' Danny, another one of Jack's soldiers and now part waiter, part chauffeur, and full-time support for whatever was going on, surprised him. It was a rare occasion when anyone managed to sneak up on him, even someone as light of feet as Danny.

'Yes?'

'There's a phone call for you. It's Sal Bernardo.'

'I'm coming.' Jack stopped himself from speculating as he hurried down the stairs, neatly dodging customers keen on being seen with White Jack Sullivan.

It was close to midnight. Uncle Sal must have a good reason to ring up the Top Note this late.

He closed the door behind him. Danny had left the light on in the office and placed the receiver on the table.

Jack lit a cigarette as he picked up phone, a habit he rarely indulged in. 'Uncle Sal? Is anything wrong?'

Uncle Sal sounded muffled. 'I might have made a clanger. My little Frances made me show her how to pick locks. She's a natural, but – '

'Damn.' Jack loosened his collar. He hadn't noticed how stuffy the air had become, despite the ceiling fan.

'I won't let her do anything,' Uncle Sal said. 'I just didn't know what to do. It did ease her mind a bit.'

'Is she asleep?'

'Out like a light.'

'I'll think of something to keep her distracted,' Jack said. 'Thanks for calling.'

He took two deep drags and stubbed out the cigarette in the ashtray. If only he'd kept his mouth shut. Now Frances wouldn't budge. Which also meant he had to return to his original glimmer of an idea and make it work. Otherwise Frances and Uncle Sal might try their hand on their own, and they were sure to be found out breaking into the office at Morphettville.

For once, Jack wished the revelers would hurry up, finish their drinks, have a last dance and swan off into the night. Instead they seemed to take an inordinate pleasure in dragging things out, while he stopped for a word here and a chin-wag there without registering much of it.

It was past two, when they closed the doors behind the last group and Jack was finally free to think. There was one other avenue worth pursuing, but again he'd need help, and that would have to wait until the morning.

The cactus had been on the lower shelf, and soft music filtered through from Dolores' apartment next door. He only hoped Phil wouldn't become an additional problem. He could swear things were serious between Dolores and her suitor, except that for an ambitious man like Phil marrying a nightclub singer could prove bad for his career. In which case Jack had to find a way to make that work. He'd known Dolores all her life, and she relied on Jack. Like Uncle Sal and Frances …

His thoughts still followed the same path, like a merry-go-round, when he fell asleep.

Marie and Bluey were already waiting when Jack came down. They lived too far from the Top Note these days, Jack thought. Even with the free use of a car, Marie's life would be easier if she could just pop in to check on her children.

Another problem he needed to think about. They piled up lately.

'Have you had breakfast?'

'Ginny made sure of that.' Jack patted Marie's hand. Ginny Barker looked after the apartments, including the cooking for Jack and Dolores. Ginny's husband Archie could manage any menial task, although he reserved his passion for the Rover roadster and the Ford sedan in the garage.

'What do we do now?' Bluey asked.

'You're still friends with Andie Miller?' Jack asked Marie.

'The babies play together all the time.' Marie

wrinkled her nose. 'I can't believe they'll both soon be three.'

'Can you pump her for information?'

'Can't you ask Phil?' Andie Miller's husband was in the police force too, but not a detective like Phil, and as a sergeant at a much lower rank.

'He's given me all he could,' Jack said. 'Invite her over and give her two tickets for our ball.'

Marie chuckled. 'That'll do the trick. What do you want me to ask her?'

'It's about the horse, if they've followed up on the owner and trainer, and if they have any idea about its real identity.'

Marie gave Andie the grand tour of the Top Note. As a young mother, her friend rarely had the chance to go out.

'It's enormous, much bigger than I remember,' Andie said. She and her husband had been among the guests at the pre-opening charity ball Jack had given in these rooms after their arrival in Adelaide, and the wireless the Millers won at the raffle that night was among Andie's most prized possessions.

'It looks different once the tables and chairs are set up. And Captain Jack insists on a decent distance between tables and stage, so you can listen to the music and still chat.'

'Unless Dolores Barden sings?' Andie twinkled. She'd been forever telling Marie that the singer would be perfect for Adelaide's radio stations, an idea that Jack seconded.

'We don't stand for rudeness.' Marie tried to keep the pride in her voice down, but she took great pleasure in the knowledge that the Top Note had high standards when it came to the way everyone on the staff was expected to be treated, from the artists to the cloak room attendant. One councilor had found that out to his chagrin, when he used his hands too freely, and Bluey chucked him out into the streets. Because they had witnesses for his behaviour, they were safe from repercussions, and word spread.

The first musicians set up their instruments. Andi gave them a longing look.

'We could sit at the back,' Marie suggested. 'I'll fetch us tea.'

'Wouldn't we be in the way?'

'As if. They love a good audience.'

Marie came back with a trolley full of tea, cake and sandwiches. The musicians could help themselves between sets. Some of them hadn't had a steady job since the last picture house had made the switch to talkies.

They picked up the tune of "Happy Days Are Here Again".

Andie snapped her fingers in tune with the music. 'They're really the cat's whiskers,' she said.

'They are,' Marie said. She crossed her fingers under the table as she went on. 'I've got a favour to ask.'

'Sure. Is it about little Bobby?'

'No, it's – you've heard about the murder at the racecourse?'

'Who hasn't?' Two thin lines crept up between Andie's brows. 'My husband says they've caught the man who did it. The vet.'

'Yeah. But what about the horse? Does he have any idea if the police have any suspects? I mean, if the horse had a false identity, someone must be behind it, just like someone must know who that horse really is. The vet couldn't have done all that by himself.'

'You want me to ask him.' Andie pondered this.

'If you can.'

'It's important to you?'

Marie had to clear her throat before she could trust her voice. 'Yeah.'

'Good-oh. I'll see what I can do.'

'Thank you.' Funny how clammy her face had become, Marie thought. She'd been prepared for more questions.

Marie found Jack in the office, in the middle of a conversation on the telephone. Frances and Uncle Sal sat side by side, both quiet as mice. Marie tried to breathe as lightly as possible.

'Yes,' Jack said into the telephone. 'No worries. I'll send someone over in a jiffy.' He hung up with a satisfied gleam in his eyes, opened the door and called, 'Bluey.'

They waited for Marie's husband.

'Yes, boss?' Bluey came running. He wiped his brow. He'd been taking care of a delivery of beer, a task that took muscle as well as the skill to tally up the number of bottles. They'd dumped one supplier unceremoniously when he'd forgotten a dozen bottles.

'I need you to drive to the racecourse.' Jack wrote out a cheque for twenty-five pounds and sealed it in an envelope addressed to Mr Dunne/Mr Lucca. 'You've just become my official assistant. Mr Lucca will show you around the facilities. I've hired their entertainment block for our ball, because of the huge demand of tickets to our charity event.'

'Got it.' Bluey took the envelope.

'Ask him for a plan to the buildings and see if you have a chance to find out how far away the stable blocks and buildings are.' Jack gave Uncle Sal and Frances a wink. 'And tell him we'll have to rehearse and would like to leave a few valuable instruments overnight, if the security is up to scratch.'

Understanding dawned in Uncle Sal's face. 'There are for sure no flies on you, Jack.'

Frances and Marie both turned to Jack for an explanation.

He said, 'How else are we supposed to find out anything if we aren't close to the action? Especially if we have to make our way into the office.'

Uncle Sal rose and took a bow. 'Signorina Francesca, this is our cue.'

Frances opened her handbag and produced a padlock, a set of handcuffs, and an assortment of weirdly shaped pins and skeleton keys. Uncle Sal held them aloft. 'Do you have a strongbox or anything else worth breaking into? Just lead me to it. I'm ready to burgle the Town Hall if it helps.'

# CHAPTER ELEVEN

*F*rances patted her wig, which together with skillful make-up and spectacles transformed her into a sharp-featured woman who could pass as a decade older than Frances's actual age. She'd be twenty-three end of November weeks, and they'd planned a huge bash at the Top Note. But not without Rob.

She fumbled again with the wig. 'Careful, or it'll slide.' Bluey said.

'It's itchy.' They had resorted to using one of the wigs left over from a New Year's show, when a trio replaced Dolores. Their dancing skills made up for the fact that their lead singer had only a passable voice compared to the Top Note's star attraction.

Pauline had taken out the waves and bobbed the wig at a sharper angle. The glossy brown was left unchanged.

Frances went through her instructions. She was grateful Jack had decided she should accompany Bluey as a secretary. Two people could cover more ground, and while Bluey might be treated with the respect befitting a man who would bring lucrative business, hardly anyone paid attention to a woman whose appearance bordered on dowdy.

She rolled down the window a couple of inches. The exhaust fumes mingled with the scent of red gums and wattle trees, now that they were outside the city centre.

Bluey steered the Rover into a spot close to the main entrance. Heat shimmered on the racecourse, and the breeze stirred up a little dust. In a few hours, galloping hooves would throw up plumes behind them, and the cries of jockeys and spectators would be audible half a mile away. For now though, an almost ethereal quiet lay over the course and the empty stands.

The large building behind showed at least a few signs of life, with a handsome thirty-something man standing at the door, a cigarette in his cupped hands.

At the back would be the stables and lodgings, Frances thought. In the blocks hidden from her sight was the room where Rob had slept, and where a murderer had snuck inside to plant evidence framing her brother.

Bluey shot her a sidewards glance. His own face was studiously blank as they left the car. Frances smoothed her frown and managed a weak smile.

The man at the door ground out his cigarette with his heel. He extended his hand and flashed them a wide smile. 'You must be Mr Sullivan's people. I'm Mike Dunne.'

Bluey shook his hand. 'Bluey Fitzpatrick, and Mr Sullivan's secretary, Miss Whitford.' They'd decided to drop the name Palmer, in case anybody made the connection with Rob. Whitford had been her mother's maiden name, making it easier to remember.

Mike Dunne gave her a brief nod as he took them inside.

Their steps clicked sharply on the concrete stairs. In the spacious passages, Frances heard only her own heels on the floorboards. The men with their rubber soles made hardly any noise, something they needed to take into account.

At the far end, a couple of gaunt jockeys handed papers to an efficient looking man with a clipboard. There must be a door close to them, leading to the stables, because Frances saw no traces of muck or straw on her side.

Mike Dunne stopped outside a door with a large fan-light and the lettering Manager in gold plate. It began level with Frances's nose and was a good fifteen inches high.

The lock was an ordinary one that opened with an ordinary barrel key. Frances's mood lightened. Inside the office, a ledger sat next to an inkwell and pen on an antique desk. The furniture looked old too, and valuable, with sumptuous brown leather armchairs. A cabinet case stood in a corner, next to a globe that would open into a liquor cabinet. Frances had seen similar models in a catalogue.

The cabinet had another simple lock. Frances wished she could see the desk drawers, but she had no reason to venture on the other side of the desk.

Bluey took out the envelope and weighed it in his hand. Mr Dunne held out his hand for it.

Frances cleared her throat, to remind Bluey of his next lines.

'I'd need a geek at the rooms first,' Bluey said with a slow chuckle. 'I'm sure it'll all be good as gold, but you know how it is.'

'Indeed. May I commend you on your business practice.' Mike Dunne's voice was as clipped and British as Frances had heard it on the wireless. It either meant he'd arrived in Australia not too long ago, maybe receiving free passage after the war, or he deliberately used it to establish his superiority.

He locked up after them.

Bluey insisted on inspecting the ball room, which would easily hold seven hundred people and a full orchestra, plus cloak rooms, washroom and a small room which could be used as a dressing room for Dolores.

Frances kept her silence. The less she talked, the smaller the risk that Mr Dunne might identify Miss Whitford as Signorina Francesca or whatever form her role would take. Instead, she wrote down all he details she could see, and the measurements. She had no idea if this information was useful in any way, but it fitted her role.

The rooms had all either recently been built or refurbished, with high ceilings, good ventilation and lighting that made them perfect for a ball.

The kitchen was smaller than Frances had expected, but the food preparation for their show was going to be done elsewhere anyway. A few of Marie's war nurse friends had banded together and ran a small catering business, with leftover food donated to the soup kitchens.

Bluey nodded his approval every minute or so. 'This is bonzer,' he finally said. 'Just right for us. That is - ' His forehead creased as if he'd hit upon a new and disagreeable thought. Frances admired his acting skills.

'Yes, Mr Fitzpatrick?'

'Call me Bluey. We'll likely see a lot of each other, with rehearsals and all that.'

Bluey ruffled his hair. 'I hate to ask it, but is your security any good? Some of these instruments would fetch a pretty penny, and the band would have to stow some of them away overnight.'

'Certainly.' Mike Dunne motioned Bluey and Frances over to a window, overlooking a low-slung stable block, with a kennel at the end. 'See that kennel?'

'Yeah.'

'Every evening from six up until I or my assistant arrive in the morning, guards make their rounds, together with highly trained dogs.'

'And during the day? It wouldn't be the first time someone tried to nobble a favourite to swing a race.'

Mike Dunne stiffened. 'Not in Morphettville, I can assure you. We have a guard on duty every day we have horses on the premises.'

'Good-oh. Miss Dolores will be happy to hear that.' Bluey patted the breast pocket with the envelope. 'How about doing the paperwork?'

He signed the document with an easy flourish that made Frances think Jack let him do more of the background work than she'd thought. She knew that Jack trusted Marie's business sense, but it appeared there was a lot more to Bluey than his physical strength and unquestioning loyalty.

The men shook hands.

'Pleasure doing business with you,' Bluey said. 'We'll be over tomorrow to set up and start preparations.' Then, as an afterthought, he extracted ten tickets to the ball from his wallet. 'For you and your men. Wives too, of course. It's going to be a beaut. The mayor and half the city's big-wigs have already announced they'll be there.'

'Can't miss that then, can we?' Mike Dunne locked away his signed copy, together with the envelope, in a desk drawer. They key was on a separate ring from the door key. He slipped it carelessly into his jacket.

'You were brill,' Frances said as soon as they eased onto the road away from the racecourse.

A faint pinkish hue appeared on Bluey's cheeks, but that could have been due to the sunlight. 'You make a fine secretary yourself,' he said. 'What did you make of the cove? Bit too posh?'

'And too keen to show us he wasn't dying to get his hands on the cheque.' Another thought occurred to her, one she couldn't bring up with Jack. 'Bluey?'

'Yeah?'

'This must all cost a fortune. I mean, hiring Morphettville and everything.' She bit her lip. She should offer to pay for the costs, but there was no way she could and still hire a lawyer.

Bluey took one giant mitt of the steering wheel to give Frances's hand a comforting squeeze. 'The captain knows what he's doing,' he said. 'Always.'

'You're right. It's just – I don't know.'

'Listen, Frances.'

Usually he called her Miss, Frances thought, putting her on a different plane from the others. She preferred it like this though.

'You've been busting your gut to take care of your family, same as what Captain Jack does now. I don't know where I and Marie and the littlees would be without him. I also know that he wouldn't think twice about doing the same for any of us.'

A warm glow enveloped Frances. 'He's pretty wonderful, isn't he?'

'Best man I've ever met, and I've seen a lot of decent men and a lot who were as crooked as a dog's hind leg. If he says, don't worry, then it'll be fine.'

Pauline waylaid Frances as she entered the cloakroom. 'You're harder to catch than a fart these days,' she said.

Frances's mouth fell open. 'Where did you get that expression from?'

'Tony. My sweetheart picked up all kinds of useful things while he was travelling.' She giggled. 'You should ask him to tell you some of his stories one day. Bring your brother along.'

So, the police report had fooled Pauline too. Frances should be happy about that, but it was a hollow victory. And Tony had trained as an architect. He could make sense of Frances's notes about Morphettville. Maybe she should tell them.

'Anyway,' Pauline went on, linking her arm with Frances's. 'Now that I've got you, I need to talk to you about my costume.'

Frances blinked in confusion.

'For the show? Honestly, Frances, what's going in with you? I thought we could have matching outfits, with lots of sequins catching the light. Mum could help.' Pauline fluttered her eyelashes at Frances. 'I've cut out a few pictures from *Everyone's*. Miss Barden gave me her old copies.'

'If Uncle Sal and Jack agree, that's fine with me.'

'You didn't have a fight, did you? Or is it your mum? You make a face like Dismal Dan.'

Frances made a quick decision. Jack would agree. 'Can you fetch Tony and meet me in Jack's office?'

'You mean, now?'

'He's still working upstairs, isn't he?'

Pauline's face took on a besotted look. 'Too right he is. That man will never leave Adelaide again, if I have to nail his coat to the rafters to keep him here.'

'I'm sure it won't come to that.' Jack had given Tony a regular job as a handyman, looking after the property he owned and cheaply rented out to his old war mates and their families.

'Although if I had known, the magazine pays you good money for your love letters, I'd made him write to me once a week while he was gone, using different names. Too late now.' Pauline swished off in a move copied from the pictures.

'Good idea, to use Tony,' Jack said. 'It's a miracle Pauline didn't catch on to the racecourse murder, but you said she won't blab.'

'She's never let me down. And she's too much in awe of you.'

They sat in the office, Frances's notes on the desk and Uncle Sal pouring over them. Marie and Bluey prepared the props for the show to be transported to the racecourse.

Pauline knocked. 'Cooee,' she sang out.

'Come in.'

Pauline nudged Tony forwards. He held his cap in his hands and twisted it. That was the only sign of unease he showed. 'Mr Sullivan. Folks.' Tony's blue eyes held theirs with a steady gaze, and he stood not too ramrod straight. After Jack and Uncle Sal, Tony was the nicest man Frances knew. Apart from Rob. A pang of fear shot through her. What if they failed?

'Take a seat,' Jack said. 'And thanks for coming.' He pushed Frances's writings over to Tony. 'Can you use these measurements and draw up a blueprint?'

'Sure,' Tony said.

'You're not building another place and leaving?' Pauline's eyes grew huge.

'It's the racecourse building,' Frances said after a small signal from Jack. 'That vet they arrested for killing a jockey is Rob, and we need to find the real murderer.'

Pauline squealed, 'Rob?' She clapped a hand over her mouth.

Tony hugged her close for a second. 'That's daft.'

'It is, but the police don't see it that way,' Jack said. 'Which is why we need your help.'

'Anything we can do.' Tony set his jaw in firm lines. 'You name it. No questions asked.'

Pauline flung her arms around Frances. 'You poor thing. How's your mum?'

'She's fine,' Uncle Sal said. 'It'll all be fine. The best brains in South Australia, eh?'

'There's one person we need to add to our suspect list,' Frances said. 'I only realised that when I saw the jockeys.'

'Who is it?'

'The doctor. Wit all those injuries, they must have a man for the human patients too. He'd know what to steal from Rob and how to use it, and the security guards wouldn't blink when they see him.'

Uncle Sal thumped the desk in his excitement. 'You're right, and I might just need to see him with my gammy ankle after a rehearsal.'

'You can lean on me,' Pauline said. 'I've always wanted to play a nurse, and a woman sees things a man wouldn't notice.'

'Excellent. The we'll all move on to Morphettville tomorrow, with Tony as our set designer.'

Pauline hugged Frances again. 'Now you stop worrying. You should have told us sooner. Have you seen Rob?'

'Once,' Frances said with a heavy heart. 'It would be too risky to visit, in case someone recognises me and puts Theodore Palmer and Frances Palmer and the Top Note together.'

'But that can also happen on the racecourse, with the same last name.'

'That's why I made you create my disguise, as Miss

Whitford. And otherwise I'm Signorina Francesca, assisting my Uncle Sal.'

'That's clever,' Pauline said. 'Tony can visit Rob. A bit of make-up, and his old clothes, and his own mother wouldn't know him.'

'Would that work?' Frances's eyes beseeched Jack. Having to accept she couldn't see Rob was the hardest part. He'd feel lonely, and deserted, and she didn't dare write him a letter if he wanted to claim he had no connection to Adelaide.

## CHAPTER TWELVE

'Open these.' Uncle Sal laid a selection of five different locks on the kitchen table. He gave his collection of oddly shaped pins and hooks a gentle pat. 'Don't forget, easy breathing, and steady does it.'

Two hours later Frances's eyes smarted, her back ached, and she had mastered the art of picking three of the locks. Uncle Sal watched her with paternal pride as she slid the hook inside the lock and gave it an ever so slight twist, waiting for the precious moment she could feel it turn. 'Done,' she said and wiped her hair out of her forehead.

Uncle Sal planted a loud kiss on her cheek. 'And now we'll do the same with the lights out.'

She was too tired to protest. Instead she found herself agreeing.

'Tomorrow,' he said. 'You need your beauty sleep, as do I. How about I make us a nice mug of cocoa?'

She had been so focused on her task, she hadn't noticed how cool the night had become, especially after the heat of the day. And how hungry she was.

'I'll do it,' she said. 'A sandwich to go with it?'

'You're reading my mind.'

They lingered over their meal, both exhausted and both unwilling to retire to their comfortable beds when Rob was forced to sleep on a prison cot.

Uncle Sal had shared enough stories about his early years in Vaudeville, when police would clamp down on travelling artists if they set so much as one foot wrong. In some places it took even less. It hadn't been Australia, if Frances remembered correctly, but the tales of wrongful imprisonment for a day or two that thrilled and scared her and Rob in equal parts in their childhood now came back to haunt her.

Judging by his somber look, they haunted Uncle Sal too. The only small mercy was the fact that they'd be careful to keep these anecdotes secret from her mother. She suffered enough already, and they'd weighed every word when they told her how well Rob kept up, and how there was no reason to worry or come back to Adelaide when Mum was needed elsewhere.

Uncle Sal pushed back his chair and rested his hand on her shoulder. 'Let's turn in.' Usually his touch was light. Not tonight though. His ankle must hurt like billy-oh, if he needed Frances to steady himself. At least tomorrow they'd try to have him seen by a doctor, murder suspect or not. And she'd ask the Chinese doctor

Jack swore by for more of his magic ointment. With all the trouble brewing, Frances had forgotten to buy a new tub of the stuff. Uncle Sal should have done it himself, but while he wouldn't mind spending his last penny on the family, he'd stint himself if it helped them.

Frances looked back over her shoulder as she followed Uncle Sal upstairs. The locks had gleamed, and there were no tell-tale scratches. He must have bought them while she was at the racecourse, pretending to be Miss Whitford.

The phone rang in the Miller household as the sergeant came down, with a shiny morning face and his uniform shirt crisp and starched.

Andie dashed to pick up. 'Hello?'

A minute later she hung up, poured tea for her husband and herself and hoped her little girl would sleep until her father was gone for the day.

There were three slices of crispy bacon on a plate. She helped herself to one of them and offered the rest to her surprised husband.

'Have I forgotten a special day?' he asked. Although with a regular salary they couldn't complain about hardship, luxuries like an extra slice of bacon were save for rare occasions.

Andie switched on the wireless. They now had several stations to choose from in Adelaide, and she fiddled with the control knob until she heard soft music. 'Do you have any idea how long it is since we last went out?'

Her husband pulled a face. 'I'm sorry, love. I could ask my mum to babysit if you want to go out for tea on my day off.'

'I've got something even better in mind.' She placed the two tickets Marie had given her next to his plate.

'What's that?' He stopped eating.

'We've been invited to the big do at the Top Note. Only it's no longer to be held at the club, because Marie says they need more space.' She gave him an irresistible smile. 'Please say we'll go.'

'We sure will, if you think my suit is up to it. Where is it to be then?'

'Morphettville racecourse.' She refilled his teacup. 'I've always wanted to see it. Just imagine to be rich enough to own a racehorse and watch it win a cup.' She sighed. 'Makes you wonder who'd do such an awful thing, to cheat and spoil people's trust.'

'It's money. People get greedy.'

'That painted horse. Have you found out its real name? I mean, the owner surely must have known.'

Her husband stirred a lump of sugar in his tea. 'It's a strange case, that one. Word on the station has it, the owner named on the papers is an eighty-year old widow from Hobart.'

'Fancy that.'

'The only trail we have is the racecourse where the

blacksmith swears he saw the gelding. He shod five nags there. But the case will probably be closed soon. It's the murder that matters, not some fraud.'

His voice sounded unconvinced, so Andie added another question.

'Do you really believe that young vet was the mastermind?'

He wiped his mouth and folded the napkin before he laid it aside. 'It's not my job to ask, but between you and me, there's something about this that gives me heartburn. Strictly between you and me.'

'Mum, Mum, Mum!' Naked feet padded along the hallway, and into the kitchen.

'There's my good girl!'

Janey hugged her father's knees. He swung her high into the air, to her squealing delight.

Andie's heart filled with happiness, as her husband placed Janey in her high-chair and kissed them both good-bye.

'Sergeant Miller, ready to protect this fair city,' he said, as he'd done for the last three years every working day.

Her response likewise hadn't changed. 'Adelaide and I rely upon you.'

She shut the door and smiled. Marie would drop off Bobby in an hour, and they'd have an interesting chin-wag ahead.

# CHAPTER THIRTEEN

*B*luey crawled on the ball room floor, drawing chalk lines wherever Tony instructed him to. Occasionally, the thunder of hooves and cry of jockeys reached their ears, thanks to opened windows. Without that, the building would be almost soundproof, with the horses hopefully undisturbed by the upcoming ball.

Frances, in her disguise as Miss Whitford, marvelled at the sheer amount of work it took to relocate from one venue to another.

Tony had drawn up plans to accommodate the bands plus Dolores on a dais. He'd also designed a swing chair for Dolores that would allow her to float through the air under a blazing chandelier. The effect should be spellbinding. At least that was the plan. If they had no earlier chance to search the office, the ball itself would be the last chance, and Dolores was the one act nobody would want to miss.

Mike Dunne had welcomed them and handed them over to his Italian assistant, Pete Lucca. Apart from his jet-black hair and pencil-thin moustache and a penchant for natty clothes, Mr Lucca looked no different from his Anglo-Saxon counterparts. Uncle Sal tried a few Italian phrases that Pete didn't understand. His parents had done their best to become proper Australians. Making sure their children spoke only English was part of that plan.

He burst with energy as he took Jack and Frances on another tour of the rooms they would use, and other rooms off-limits to them. Since these were only maintenance and tack rooms, apart from the stable blocks, Frances didn't mind.

'Here's our doctor's practice.' Pete knocked on a wooden door with a hard-worn rush mat outside it. When no answer came, he said, 'Our doc spends most hours with the jockeys. One or two of them always manage to bust themselves up.'

'Is he only working days?' Jack scratched his chin. 'We can't afford anyone to take a tumble and no doctor around. I'll have to bring one from town, then.'

'No need for that. If he has a patient who needs more than a bandage and an aspirin, he stays overnight. If you offer him a few quid, he'll be all yours.'

'I appreciate that,' Jack said. 'Are you here every day?'

'The boss is doing a lot of business in town, and he travels a lot,' Pete said. 'Do you have any idea how many racing and turf clubs there are in Australia? Hundreds.'

Jack whistled through his teeth. 'And they all work together?'

'Depends on who and where, but, yeah, it's a big job. And our cup alone is one of Australia's biggest race days. We're not Fremont in Melbourne, but we're holding our own.'

They trotted back to the ball room, Frances a step behind the men in her role as overlooked woman.

'Pity when there's a whiff of scandal,' Jack said. 'Or is it good for business?'

Did Pete stiffen for a heartbeat?

'Nothing has been proven about the horse, if that's what you're driving at,' he said. 'Morphettville has one of the cleanest records everywhere.'

'I think it's amazing how you tell all these horses apart.' Frances lowered her voice by half an octave.

'There are records for every single racer, with their age, height, colours and so on. But of course, it's impossible to make sure there is no fraud attempt at all. Same as you can't be sure about humans.'

'That's right,' Jack said. 'Back in '19, there was one woman who cashed in from the Repat for three injured sons. They'd all looked alike, apart from the odd difference. No-one doubted her until a clever bloke took a close look at the files and wondered about them all losing the right leg and catching a lung full of gas.'

'Despicable,' Pete said. He unlocked the office door. 'Give me a shout if you need anything.'

'Thanks,' Jack said.

Bluey and Tony were almost finished.

Pauline and Uncle Sal put the wheeled chair together. They'd built a second one, because at Morphettville, they would rehearse without Signorina Francesca as target. Playing one role would be difficult enough, and Frances needed to be around as Jack's secretary.

They'd rehearse with her back at the Top Note.

'What do you say?' Tony stepped back to show them his layout. The dais would be high enough to allow an observer to keep an eye out for anyone passing by, on their way to and from the office. 'Good enough for Miss Whitford to sit and take notes?'

Jack lifted Frances in the air, taking her by surprise. 'This is about the height we could achieve without being obvious,' he said.

She peered through the transom window. Lucky for them, Morphettville had sprung for clear glass. At the right angle she could see enough of the hallway to cover that approach to the office. If someone came along using the back entrance, they needed another observation spot.

'It works,' she said. 'But only for this side.'

Jack gently lowered her again. 'We're having the cloak room scrubbed and manned. Tony'll do it once we've set up here.'

'Tony?' Pauline stared at her fiancé. 'Maybe I should do it.'

He grinned at her. 'With all these men running around, I don't think so. Besides, Rob's my mate too.'

'It would be good to know how many staff we're talking about,' Jack said. 'The kitchen team should have an idea.'

'Marie will take care of that,' Bluey said. He pushed himself into an upright position and wiped the chalk off his hands. 'She can get anyone to talk, that woman can.'

'True.' Jack pointed at Bluey's knees. 'You better dust yourself off before you pick her up.'

Bluey patted a cloud of chalk dust off his clothes.

They'd hired a delivery van to transport props, instruments and, once the set-up was complete, the musicians.

Currently it stood outside the entrance, with a grand piano and a drum set yet to be brought in. Once that was done, Bluey would return to town to fetch Marie for a quick run-through. They'd agreed to leave her at home or at the Top Note as much as possible. Apart from minding her children, even with the aid of parents, there was also the day to day business of the club, and Dolores needed company as well, to keep her thoughts off everything that could go wrong.

Realistically, they all couldn't afford to spend more than a few hours a day at Morphettville, so they had to be creative.

# CHAPTER FOURTEEN

*M*arie appeared as Jack and Uncle Sal nailed the last boards for the dais into place. All they needed now was three steps leading up to it. It made it easier for the musicians to climb up, and it allowed Dolores a dramatic moment when she would shimmy up to the microphone and down again.

The swing chair would be tested at the Top Note and brought over at a later date. Pauline had volunteered to try it out, in case something went wrong. If Dolores so much as twisted an ankle, they'd be in trouble.

Marie brought cold pies and salads, which she dished up before she sought out the kitchen to make tea, a cloth-covered basket in her hand. Frances went along, to help. She hoped for a quiet moment to chat. She practiced Miss Whitford's voice, and her walk as well, and using it on Marie would be as good as a dress rehearsal.

One rosy-cheeked cook and her elderly helper, a former jockey judging by his diminutive stature and slight whiff of stable, prepared food in the kitchen. The cook stirred a stew, and the man peeled potatoes.

Frances knocked on the open door, to announce them.

'Hello?' Marie beamed at the kitchen staff. 'That smells bonzer.'

The cook inhaled the stew fragrance. 'Not bad, if I say so myself. You with the fancy outfit?'

'I promise we'll do out best not to get in the way,' Frances said. 'We were hoping to boil the kettle, that's all.'

'And to introduce ourselves.' Marie lifted the cloth off the basket. 'I've brought sponge cake and a fruit loaf.'

The helper's gaze fell greedily upon the offerings.

The cook caught his interest and guffawed. 'Look at that poor toad. Twenty years of hardly a morsel, and he's still making up for it.'

'As long as he can appreciate his food now.' Marie twinkled at them both as she and Frances set their offerings on the work bench. She filled a kettle and put it on a small stove away from the big range the cook was using. 'It must be hard to serve up a stew like this, and no-one allowed to enjoy it the way he would.'

'Too right it is. But at least there's some having more than one bite.' The cook wiped her hands on her apron and took a knife out of a drawer. With deft movements, she sliced the fruit loaf into even pieces of about an inch.

'I hope I've made enough for everyone,' Marie said.

Frances forgot to breathe while she waited for the answer.

'That'll do us for sure,' the cook said. 'Like I said, the jockeys don't eat much, for fear they'll get too heavy, and then there's only a dozen stable lads and trainers, the doctor, and the office staff who eat cake.' She patted her stomach. 'It'll go down a treat if it's half as good as it looks.'

'I've met Mr Dunne and Mr Lucca,' Frances said. 'Do they have lots of assistants?'

'One typist, and an accountant,' the cook said. 'And occasionally we have additional typists coming from the employment agencies to help with the busiest times, like Christmas.'

The kettle boiled. Marie filled the two thermos canisters she'd brought in the basket. 'I hope you don't mind us popping in now and then.'

'You're always welcome,' the cook said. 'Nice to have new people to chat with.' She lowered her voice. 'It's not easy as the only female around, believe me.'

'I can imagine.' Marie smiled as Frances took the basket.

Frances had to remind herself to keep up Miss Whitford's brisk, efficient gait. Inwardly, she felt like skipping. She'd feared a list of staff a mile long. Instead, they had less than twenty names they needed to find out. If they had those, they could start whittling them down once the racing programmes from Jack and Bluey's connections arrived.

She paused.

'What's wrong?' Marie gave her a concerned look.

'The colicky horse,' Frances said. 'Rob was worried sick about him.'

'Leave it to me.' Marie deposited the thermos canisters in the basket and hurried to the kitchen.

'It's me again,' Frances heard her say. 'I've got a cousin in the country whose horse got into the apple orchard. That can be dangerous for an animal, right?'

Frances didn't hear the answer, because it would have looked too peculiar to stand like a statue in the hallway, the basket in her hand.

Marie took only a few moments to follow her.

'Smoke-oh,' Marie called out as soon as they were back. She set out cups and saucers and filled them with strong tea.

'What did the cook say?' Frances asked.

'The horse is fine. They haven't had an animal die since one of them broke a leg on the home stretch.'

'That's good.' A little of the tension in Frances's stomach melted away. Knowing he'd saved his patient would cheer Rob up. Tony would see him in the afternoon, when Bluey would take them all home.

'How does it work?' Frances asked as she removed her wig. Her own hair was matted underneath and sticky with sweat.

'How does what work?' Jack slip open a thick brown envelope and shook it. Out fell a wad of racing programmes.

'That.' Frances picked up the first one. Fremont racecourse, Easter 1930. A note in pencil said, *winner race five, day one, odds 125 to two.* 'The betting. Do you have to be there in person, or can you phone up, or send a note?'

'In which case you wouldn't have to be there.' Jack gave her a quick kiss, something he didn't do too often in public.

'On the other hand, if you have to be there, the bookie who sold the betting slip planted in Rob's room, would recognise him.' She massaged her scalp. She needed a shower, after she'd finished her meandering train of thoughts.

'Because no-one could claim he'd have risked sending another person in his stead, especially since they all thought he was a newcomer to Adelaide.' Jack's eyes sparkled. 'You're absolutely right.'

Uncle Sal had listened in silence. Now he chimed in. 'If the slip is real, and not a fake.'

'I don't understand,' Frances said.

'Well, as soon as the hullaballoo started, people

would look dodgy with those huge wins on a nag that should have come in last. You'd throw them away, wouldn't you? Or tear 'em up or burn 'em.' Uncle Sal's gaze travelled from Frances to Jack. 'It would be good to have a gander at that slip, or Tony could ask Rob if he remembers which bookie it was from. It would also be good to have an idea which bookies sold bets on the painted horse.'

Frances hugged Uncle Sal. 'You're the smartest, most wonderful man in the world.'

Uncle Sal winked at Jack. 'Don't you forget that when these young fellows come along.'

'I'm no match for you,' Jack said. 'The question is, who do we sound out, without setting off alarm-bells?'

'I wish the police would do their job.' Frances stuck out her bottom lip. It might be unfair to Phil, but he could have done more.

'Who would a bookmaker talk to?' she asked.

'Not the police, or any busybody.' Jack waved Bluey closer. 'There must be a place where they go for a snort or two on race days. Probably a hotel with a licence.' Since bona fide travellers could in certain establishments still legally drink alcohol after six o'clock, the number of travellers had exploded.

'I could suss them out,' Bluey said.

'You're too well known, and too easily recognisable,' Jack said.

Frances agreed. At over six foot, with a boxer's

physique and his red thatch, Bluey stood out in any crowd.

'Uncle Sal on the other hand is a master of disguise. How good are you as an actor?'

Uncle Sal hunched his shoulders and took a little bow. His voice took on a lilting quality as he said, 'Top of the morning to you.'

'An Irish-man.' Jack nodded his approval.

'Doon Connemara way, with t' gift of the gab.' Uncle Sal smoothed his salt-and-pepper hair. 'A boy of grey powder and rubber inlays for my cheeks, and you won't know me from Adam.'

'Bluey will sit in a quiet corner, to keep an eye on you,' Jack said. 'We only have eight days left until the ball.'

Eight days! An iron fist clenched Frances's heart.

Uncle Sal gave her a comforting back rub. 'I'm sorry you can't come along, my darling.'

'That's okay,' Frances forced herself to say. 'I'll search through the programmes while you're gone.'

'Until then, how about we rehearse our number before Pauline needs to assist Dolores?' Uncle Sal whispered into Frances's ear. 'It's hard, but we need to keep the show going, or Jack will lose his customers.'

Frances looked at him in a slight shock. She hadn't even thought of that. Of course, the Top Note would only be closed for the night of their ball at the racecourse. They had to fit in their investigation with the rehearsals and the day-to-day running of their ordinary affairs.

Frances could count herself lucky to have these days off. Her friends didn't have that luxury.

'I'll get changed,' she said. She needed to be in her full gear, otherwise Uncle Sal couldn't take the size of her blonde wig and her dress in account when he flung his knives.

Pauline strapped her roller skates to her feet. Her eyes glittered with excitement. Her friend lived for these moments in the limelight, Frances thought with a pang.

'Uncle Sal?'

'Yes, my darling?'

'If I would swap places with Pauline -' She couldn't finish her sentence because Pauline squeezed her so tight, she could barely breathe.

'Please, please, please say yes, Uncle Sal.' Pauline had stars in her eyes as she eased her death-grip on Frances. Tony's jaw dropped for an instant, although he recovered remarkably well.

'You understand it's a bit risky?' Uncle Sal asked.

'Not if you use these.' Jack grabbed a knife from the table and threw it at Uncle Sal. The old man ducked, and the knife landed in the wall.

Frances gasped.

Uncle Sal pulled the knife out of the wall. Miraculously, it had left no marks. He tested it with his thumb. The gleaming blade slipped back into the hilt.

'Theatrical props,' Uncle Sal said. 'I haven't seen this quality since the London Palladium.'

'They only arrived this morning. Can you use them?'

'Oh yes, my boy. I'll make it look just as good as if I used the real ones.'

Pauline looked doubtful. Tony let out a big sigh of relief.

'That's sorted,' Jack said. 'Ready to go to prison, Tony?'

# CHAPTER FIFTEEN

*U*ncle Sal shuffled into the tavern. An oversized shabby jacket, a soft cap and a little make-up had transformed him from a dapper gentleman into an ageing worker, like thousands of others. He blended in with the surroundings, where people came for a quick snort to celebrate or to commiserate, while constantly on the look-out for police.

The path to the backdoor was kept clear and could be reached within seconds from the rough-hewn tables and the proper bar.

Bluey had his head buried in a racing programme, and a soft hat covered his hair. He'd ordered a pint of beer as well as a pint of lemonade which gave him a cover should an officer of the law turn up.

Uncle Sal sat on a bar stool next to a trio of slick coves. At least two of them were bookies, because they

143

congratulated themselves on making good money on favourites who'd lost by a nose.

Uncle Sal liked to hear that. Losing by a few inches was impossible to calculate. He'd read enough about thrown races in the United States to hope this kind of crime wouldn't catch in Australia. Painted horses were bad enough, but organised crime would be the end of horse-racing.

He lifted his glass and managed to accidentally elbow the fellow next to him.

'Watch it.' The man glared at him, more out of habit than annoyance. It had been a gentle touch, with no harm done.

'Sorry,' Uncle Sal said. 'What a clumsy chap I am.' He threw a handful of money n the counter. 'A round of the same for these gentlemen.'

'Well, I'm not saying no to that,' the bookie next to Uncle Sal said. 'That's mighty generous of you.'

Sal swigged his beer and wiped his mouth. His chin sprouted convincing white stubbles, thanks to his experience on the stage. 'I had me a bit of good luck with the nags, and why not spread the cheer while we can, eh?'

'I drink to that,' his new friend that.

'I wish I'd been at the races last week, but there you are. I missed that excitement. I'd had an eye on that gelding myself. Plain brown ones without any markings have always been good to old Bernie.' Uncle Sal chuckled to himself.

'That bloody horse.' The bookie beetled his brows. 'That's the kind of thing gives us bookmakers all a bad name.'

'But it'd cost you a nice packet, wouldn't it, if somebody placed a whole lot of cash on a filly nobody else looks at?'

'Yeah. But the public ain't that smart, are they?'

'The next time I want a little flutter, can I phone it in?' Uncle Sal asked. 'It's hard to give up an arvo at the races, but if I say no to a day's work, my daughter won't let me hear the end of it.'

'With some you can, with others, no.'

The man next to him broke his silence. 'I like to see a face when I do business. You know, get a feel if a joker's likely to bail out when he sees a man in uniform.'

'It's sad when it comes to painted horses in Adelaide.' Uncle Sal sighed in his beer.

'Next thing it's the bloody mob. All these Italians and Irish, stands to reason if they go crook in America, they go crook here.'

'Hey,' Sal's new friend said, offended. 'My mum's Italian, and she's in and out of the church so much my dad barely sees her.'

'I'm not saying it's all of them,' the other man said. 'But it doesn't take many rotten apples to spoil the barrels. Look at the Germans. I mean, there was a reason to lock so many up on Kangaroo Island when we were at war.'

'Like my uncle, you mean?' The third bookie slammed his hand on the bar counter.

Bluey left his table and planted himself on a bar stool.

Sal hastened to change the subject before a serious brawl broke out.

'But you'd have noticed if there as anything up with the fillies,' he said. 'Nobody'd know better than you if something felt wrong.'

'That's right.' The second bookie was calm again. 'And I swear, there was nothing.'

'What about the second race meeting of the year? When that mare cost us a few hundred quid each? Never won a race before, and then leaving the other nags standing?' The first bookie snorted.

'Probably a brown one, with no markings. I told you, they're always in the money.' Sal chuckled.

'She had one white stocking.'

'Then I wouldn't have picked her. You didn't have to fork out for that painted horse, did you?' Sal swigged his beer.

The first bookie groaned. 'Don't mention it. There's no proof the horse was a wrong 'un, they said. Only the blacksmith's word, and with him gone, we were proper in the soup.'

'It must have been awful to find out you took a bet from a murderer,' Sal said. 'Did it give you the creeps when that young vet handed over his money? My grandmother always swore the hairs on her neck stood

146

up when a bad one crossed her path. Had the second sight, my grandmother did.'

'I never saw him.' The first bookie looked at his mates. They both shook their heads.

Uncle Sal finished his beer. 'See you around, gentlemen.'

He hunched up his shoulders as he shuffled away. The odds were slim the men would see him again, but he wouldn't want even the smallest thing to connect the fictious Bernie with Salvatore Bernardo.

Bluey followed at a leisurely pace. He'd parked the Rover well-hidden from sight, and there was no-one around as he unlocked the door. Just in case he was mistaken he asked, 'Can I give you a lift, mate?'

'Thanks a million,' Uncle Sal said as he climbed in. 'You're a real prince, you are.'

# CHAPTER SIXTEEN

*U*ncle Sal all but danced into the Top Note. Bluey had a grin like the Cheshire Cat. Frances, who had been practicing her roller-skating around the tables with a grim determination, stopped so abruptly she had to steady herself by holding on to something. Or in this case, someone.

Jack staggered back as she grabbed his arm. He instinctively enclosed her in an embrace, to prevent her from falling. She stooped to take off the skates. 'Tell me you've found out who did it,' she said to Uncle Sal.

'I wish. But we did find out a whole lot,' Uncle Sal said. 'Where's Tony?'

'He should be back soon,' Jack said as he released Frances.

They filed into his office, so the main room could be readied for another night.

Tony came in a little later, his breath smelling of beer.

A lump formed in Frances's throat. Tony hardly ever touched alcohol, especially not before he'd had his evening meal. A nerve twitched in his jaw.

'How's Rob?' she asked. Her voice came out in a whisper.

Jack slung his arm around her and held her tight.

'He's good.' Tony cleared his throat. 'Really. All he cared about was that horse he'd treated, and to let you know you're not to worry.'

'Then why do you look as if you've seen your grandmother's ghost?' Uncle Sal asked.

Tony gave Frances a quick glance.

'Whatever it is, you can say it,' she said.

'It's just, we used to make up stories about the prison when we were boys. And today, seeing people stroll along North Terrace, when there are these poor sods locked up a few steps away ...' He shook himself. 'I don't make sense. But Rob is good.'

Jack took a bottle of brandy and a shot glass from a shelf. He poured Tony a small snifter. 'This'll help chase the ghosts away.'

'Meanwhile Bluey and I have found a real clue,' Uncle Sal said. 'Unless there's a lot of hopeless horses around who suddenly figure out how to run, we had a painted horse on our track in January. Second race day of the year. When Rob was with his family in Queensland.'

149

Frances eyes felt moist. 'That proves it, doesn't it? We should tell Phil.'

'Not so fast.' Jack handed her his tissue. 'Even if we could show fraud, which we can't, it doesn't make it impossible in the eyes of the police for Rob to pull the same trick. But it gives us a lot of starting points, as soon as we identify that horse.'

'Sal and I have been chewing on it,' Bluey said. 'All we need to do is send Marie to the newspaper office and have her look at the paper. It would have made a splash if an unknown racer wins.'

'I could do it,' Frances said.

Jack shook his head. 'The less you're seen as yourself or as Miss Whitford, the better. Marie will buy copies for the whole fortnight. We don't want anyone to twig on to the fact we're interested in the races at all.'

He gave Frances a quick smile. 'There's plenty to do for you.'

'Mr Dunne? Mr Lucca?' Frances knocked on the office door. There was no answer. She pressed on the door handle. As expected, the office was locked.

She strode towards the accountant's office on the second floor. The rapid clacks of a mechanical calculator were the only sound inside. Frances gazed out of the window. Half a dozen men led horses around the green, probably in preparation for a final training. Would a jockey really not remember a horse, or would they keep quiet for fear of losing their job?

She knocked on this door as well.

'Come in,' a male voice said. She found the owner in a dim corner, a grey-haired man hunched over his machine. Green light filtered through drawn blinds. It gave the accountant a sickly face-colour.

Opposite him, a male typist about Frances's own age attacked the keyboard with abandon. Since Frances hadn't heard the typewriter before, she assumed the sudden outburst of activity had a lot to do with her appearance.'

'I'm sorry to disturb you,' she said. 'I'm Mr Sullivan's secretary, and I wondered where we could make a few phone calls.' She had expected to see a telephone in this office, but unless it was hidden away in the unopened section of the roll top desk on which the calculator stood, she'd been mistaken.

The accountant blinked at her. His eyes were rimmed with the pink caused by a sensitivity, which would explain the drawn blinds.

'The Top Note? We have hired your facilities for a charity ball,' Frances said.

The typist's face lit up. 'Smashing, eh, Henry?'

'It's Mr Henry to you, thank you very much.'

The typist gave him a cheeky grin in reply.

Mr Henry ignored him studiously as he addressed Frances. 'We currently only have the one apparatus available.'

The typist lifted a frayed cable off the floor. 'Wiring's got a bit haywire.' He laughed at his own harmless pun.

A likeable lad, Frances decided, a bit like an overgrown puppy. Mr Henry was the same, more bark than bite.

'And that one apparatus would be where?' She tapped on her handbag, hoping to convey the notion that she had lots of important things to take care of.

'The manager's office,' Mr Henry said.

'Which was empty.' She sighed.

The typist emphasised the mister as he said, 'Mr Henry's got a spare key.'

'For emergencies only. Which this situation does not fall under. Mr Lucca's out for today, but Mr Dunne should be here any moment.' His tone implied that the case was closed.

Frances peered around. 'Could I set up my typewriter here? I'd work downstairs, but it's hard for the performers to concentrate when I'm typing letters.'

'We have a spare machine you could use,' Mr Henry said.

'If you're sure?'

'Leave it to us, and we'll see you right. After lunch?'

'Thank you.' Frances closed the door behind her and took a deep breath. That was easier than she'd expected.

She heard movement in the manager's office and saw the

top of a dark head through the transom window in the door. She rapped on the door and pressed the handle. It was still locked.

Dissonant whistles behind her back startled her. The doctor, she reckoned after a glimpse at well-scrubbed hands and a black medical bag, not unlike Rob's.

Tony and Bluey heaved the grand piano onto the dais. The musicians would arrive at noon. Despite her preoccupation with her brother, Frances knocked on wood. This had to be the highlight of Adelaide's events, for all their sakes.

Pauline gave her a finger wave, her wrists and ankles stuck in the holds Tony had created. Marie ran in circles, pushing Uncle Sal's wheeled chair while counting under her breath to stick with the same speed.

Uncle Sal flung the theatrical knives with an easy flair, while Pauline tried hard not to flinch.

Tony gulped visibly.

Frances took pity on him. 'It's really safe,' Frances said. 'Even if Uncle Sal would miss, which he doesn't. Ever.'

Tony wiped his brow. 'She'd bite my head off if I said a word against it. I want Pauline to have fun, but it's hard to relax with all this crazy stuff going on. What if the mur-'

Frances clapped a hand over his mouth. 'Quiet. You never know who listens.' She looked around. 'Where is Jack?'

'He's getting ready to go back to the Top Note with Marie.' Tony winked at her. 'About some paperwork.'

Jack came back together with the musicians. Jack pressed a handwritten list with a dozen names in Frances's hand. 'Those letters,' he said in a tone that spoke of easy command. 'I need them first thing.'

'Yes, Mr Sullivan.'

Frances made her way upstairs. Mr Henry and the typist had been as good as their word. A portable Underwood and a stack of paper waited on a small table set against the wall.

She placed her notebook and a pencil on the desk and inserted a sheet of paper into the machine. Thankfully she'd learned how to type a few years ago, and after mastering the lightning-quick movements a switchboard operator needed, playing her role here should be easy.

She'd typed two letters and studied her fake shorthand in the notebook with as much concentration as she could without overdoing it, when Mr Henry finally declared it lunch time.

Frances inserted a fresh sheet.

'Aren't you coming?' he asked.

She gazed up, seemingly lost in her work. 'Oh. I'd rather finish my letters. They're urgent, but, thank you.'

He held up his keychain.

The young typist tugged at Mr Henry's sleeve. 'It'll be fine.'

Frances could have hugged him.

'I promise I won't leave the office unattended,' she said.

Mr Henry gave in, as she'd hoped. 'We'll be back in half an hour.'

Frances waited until she heard them clatter down the stairs with their hobnailed shoes. She swiftly moved over to Mr Henry's desk. An accountant should have the payroll, with the names of the employees.

He'd locked his desk. Frances fished in her handbag for the small velvet roll she kept her lock-picks in, to prevent their clinking.

Her pulse raced as she inserted the first hook in the lock. She forced herself to breathe in a steady, slow rhythm, the way Uncle Sal taught her. Faint movement in the lock rewarded her. She pushed the roll top up, as a soft cough outside the door alarmed her.

She dropped the roll top, slipped the lock-picks inside her blouse and kneeled on the floor.

'What are you doing?' Mr Henry asked. He trod softly towards her, so only the typist had tell-tale loud shoes.

'You gave me a start there,' she said and held out her hand. In her palm, she held a button she'd torn off her blouse cuff. 'I must have caught it on the machine.'

He moved over to his desk. Frances told herself not to panic. He picked up a spectacle case. 'The doctor said I should not go out in the sun without these.'

'What are they?'

He snapped the case open. Inside lay a pair of spectacles with dark lenses.

'Oh, sun shades,' she said, 'I've seen them in *Everyone's*. But I mustn't keep you.' She cringed at her words. Would Miss Whitford, this epitome of efficency and business-sense read that magazine and look at the screen star section? Then again, why not?

Frances counted to one hundred after Mr Henry had left before she returned to burgling his desk.

## CHAPTER SEVENTEEN

he moment Mr Henry and the typist reappeared, Frances clutched her stack of letters and her handbag. 'You've been most kind,' she said as she stepped out of the office, a list of names secreted inside her bag.

She'd have to wait until they were safely back at the Top Note before they could use it, but she'd done it.

Now they only had one more trick to pull off.

While a trumpeter blew a solo in "I Can't Give You Anything But Love", Uncle Sal swept Pauline into his arms for a dance. One false step though, and he audibly gasped in pain.

'What's wrong?' Pauline's huge eyes and her trembling lips would have done any silent era actress proud, Frances thought.

'It's nothing.' Uncle Sal clenched his teeth as he rubbed his ankle.

The musicians stopped.

'Please, gentlemen, go on,' Frances said, secretly pleased that none of them had made the connection between Signorina Francesca and the hitherto unknown Miss Whitford.

To Uncle Sal, she said, 'I'll take you to the doctor.'

Pauline had reluctantly agreed it would be better if Frances played that part too. At least she still had her starring role at the ball itself.

Uncle Sal limped so dramatically, Bluey half-carried him. Frances went ahead. The doctor's door stood ajar.

'Hello?' she called out.

'One moment,' someone answered. A jockey with a pinched face and a bandaged wrist came out. He shot her a curious glance but lost interest half-way through giving her the once-over. The slight padding Pauline had added to Frances's waist worked well in making her invisible.

Blue and Frances took a pale Uncle Sal inside.

The doctor, a middle-aged man with a red-veined nose, swivelled around on his desk chair. Flush against one wall stood a medicine cabinet with glass doors. The key stuck in the lock, A set of drawers labelled "Medical Instruments" and an examination bed half hidden by a folding screen completed the surgery set-up. 'You one of those night-club fellows?'

Uncle Sal gave him a wan smile. 'Salvatore Bernardo, at your service.'

'It's his ankle,' Frances said. 'He's one of our main performers, and we need him back on both feet, Doctor.'

'O'Leary.' The doctor motioned Uncle Sal to walk around.

Uncle Sal's stifled groans deserved a bigger audience, Frances thought.

'Sit down and remove shoe and sock.'

Bluey hurried to help Uncle Sal.

Frances averted her gaze. The ankle was criss-crossed with scars, and lumpier than it should be thanks to the steel plate that held together once splintered bone. A boozy driver was responsible for that and the end of Uncle Sal's stage career.

'Can you circle the foot?' the doctor asked.

Uncle Sal gripped the side of the bed as he tried to move his ankle. He gave up after two inches.

Dr O'Leary probed flesh and bones with his fingers. 'Nothing dislocated, but with an injury this bad you will always be laid up a wee while after a wrong step.' He unlocked the cabinet, took out a jar with an ointment reeking of eucalyptus and rubbed it on Uncle Sal's ankle, before he bandaged it tightly.

'I've strapped it up as much as possible. Any more, and it'll cut off your blood circulation. If you stay off your feet for a day or two, you should see improvement. When's your big day?'

'In a week,' Uncle Sal said.

'That'll do you easily.' Dr O'Leary's gaze shifted to a bottle at the back of the cabinet.

'Do you have fixed hours?' Bluey asked. 'In case we have another accident.'

'I'm here during training and races. If you come a cropper when I'm not here, send someone around. I live a few minutes up the road.'

He wrote an address and a telephone number on a piece of paper and handed it to Bluey.

Uncle Sal made a huge show of leaning on Bluey's arm as he limped towards the car.

Pauline and Tony were already waiting. The musicians could rehearse on their own for a few hours.

'How was the doctor?' Pauline asked. 'A dish or a crook?' She fluttered her eyelashes at Tony.

'Were you planning on handing me back my ring?' he asked.

She snuggled up against his shoulder. 'Never. I was just thinking, if he's a dish, Miss Barden might want a crack at him. She's missing out on all the fun.' Pauline stopped herself, aghast. 'Not that there's anything funny about Rob's being in prison now, but once he's cleared -'

Tony shut his sweetheart's mouth with a firm hand.

Jack was busy with his accounts, when they arrived, but

Marie waved at them with a handful of newspaper clippings.

Jack glanced up and pushed his ledger aside. 'You're early.'

'Fast work today, boss,' Bluey said.

Frances fished out her illicitly gotten list and added it to Marie's notes.

'So, you got them,' Jack said.

'It wasn't that hard.' She pulled out the pins hat held her wig in place. 'At least, the lock-picking wasn't. Mr Henry almost caught me.'

Jack's jawline tightened.

'It's okay,' she said. 'I'll be more careful next time.' Scary as it had been, she'd also felt invigorated.

'And the doctor?'

'He likes his drink,' Bluey said. 'Not a heavy boozer, I'd say, but close.'

'He had a bottle of sly-grog hidden in his medicine cabinet, and he's chewing gum to mask the smell.' Uncle Sal grimaced.

'I didn't notice that,' Frances said.

'How could you?' Uncle Sal stroked her hand. 'Well-stocked cabinet too, and he had the key in the lock.'

'But the blacksmith was killed with things from Rob's bag,' Frances said.

'Which were easy to get hold of because Rob had a patient. If he hadn't, a sedative in his tea would have worked.'

'You're saying the doctor stays on our suspect list.' Jack made a note on Frances's list.

'He wore expensive shoes,' Uncle Sal said. 'Hand-made, is my guess.'

'We haven't been sitting around either,' Marie said. Her eyes sparkled with excitement.

'The newspaper?' Frances picked up the clippings. They all dealt with races, and Marie had underlined some names.

'The horse in question is called Miss Molly and was supposed to be a novice. Nothing remarkable during the one training session the sports reporter saw, and the jockey is described as being as surprised as the rest when she took off like the clappers.' Marie made a dramatic pause. 'According to the articles, the owner of this remarkable racer is an old lady called Josephine Cowper, in Hobart. Same as with Alfie.'

## CHAPTER EIGHTEEN

'You realise what that means?' A slow, lazy grin spread over Jack's face. 'We have a pattern, and a name, Mrs Cowper.' He and Marie exchanged a triumphant look.

Frances had trouble figuring out the importance.

Marie took pity on her. 'There is no way a woman in her eighties is running a game with the fillies. But since her name and address appear to be real, our crims must be closely connected to her. Either they forged her signature, or they do business for her.'

Now Frances understood. 'There'll be paperwork in Mr Lucca's office. Maybe it gives us more information.'

'I'll do it,' Uncle Sal said.

'No. It's easier for me, as the secretary, in case we trip up.'

'We might not even need that,' Marie said. 'I grew up

163

in Tassie, and my aunt promised me to do a bit of digging. Hobart's a small enough place.'

'Then we didn't need my list?'

Jack touched her cheek. 'It's our best shot yet to see if there are connections between people and racecourses. Trainers, stable hands, jockeys, all the people who have easy access and information. And then there's the vet. It'll be interesting to see who your brother replaced.'

'Maybe he retired,' Frances said. 'Or the travelling became too much.'

'Possible, kiddo. But it could also be a case of the jitters. If he talks, that's fine. But I don't think he will, which will tell us a lot more.'

'Because he'd be afraid of what happens.'

Jack nodded. 'We'll leave the name checking to Marie while you and Uncle Sal rehearse, and I keep the Top Note humming.'

Frances spun around in a figure of eight. Her skating skills came back, but not fast enough for her liking. She needed to shut out thoughts about anything else or she stumbled. That might end with skinned knees during rehearsals but would ruin the performance if it happened on stage.

Uncle Sal clapped in sync with the speed they'd have to use for the show as she spun, circled, reversed and finally came to a halt in front of him.

Pauline eyed Frances's skates with fond nostalgia. 'Wouldn't it be bonzer if we could do that routine in the Top Note too? It's too much fun for just one night.'

'Then you'd have to give up working for Dolores,' Frances reminded her friend.

'No way.' Pauline adored doing the singer's hair and acting as her dresser.

Uncle Sal glanced at his watch. 'We've got half an hour left. Even if it's for one night only, you need to take your place.'

Frances broke into a sweat as she twirled Uncle Sal's chair around. Despite the fan, her clothes clung to her skin as the air grew soggier.

For one crazy moment she toyed with the idea of changing into one of Dolores old frocks, don her wig and visit the prison, if only to see that they had some form of relief from the heat for the prisoners. But she couldn't, and she had no way of knowing how Rob really fared.

Tony might believe that her brother was in good spirits. She knew better. Their uncle was a policeman, and they had been raised in the knowledge that evil would be punished with all the might of the law. The only thing they hadn't learned on their mother's knees was that innocent people could just as easily be entangled as guilty ones.

Every inch of Rob's skin crawled. It was nerves, he told

himself, and the heat that soaked his clothes in clammy sweat. He counted himself lucky his wife and small son couldn't see him reduced to this. He tried to have faith in the system, and in his sister, but his hopes sank a little more with every passing hour. The evidence looked too convincing.

As a schoolboy, he and Tony had listened to the tolls of the prison bell when convicted wife murderer Alexander Lee was taken to the gallows. The ringing went on for two minutes, and the two boys had mimed the slipping of the noose over the convict's head and his slow choking to death. The memory of their own cruelty made him feel sick. Adelaide had stopped the ominous bell ringing, so if the worst happened, he had the small comfort that his family wouldn't have that sound etched into their memories.

He hugged his knees. If he wanted to stay sane, he needed to concentrate. Was there anything or anyone at Glen Yarra racecourse where he and the blacksmith had met? Maybe if he went over every step he could remember, it would help his case.

Jack sent Uncle Sal and Frances home after a quick dinner. They both could do with a rest, especially Frances. Uncle Sal had promised to slip a mild sleeping draught into her tea, to stop her from tossing around half the night again.

He toured the Top Note, half of his mind on making sure ball room, dining alcoves and everything else was up to his exacting standards, the other half occupied with solving the case in the week they still had access to Morphettville.

'Wipe that frown off your face or you'll scare the customers away.'

Dolores' appearance startled him. He should have noticed her, or the sharp clicking of her heels and the heady scent of her French perfume.

He lifted the corners of his mouth. 'You're right.'

'Is it that bad?' she asked.

'We're dealing with a very smart person,' Jack said. 'Not too greedy, or he wouldn't have been able to resist placing ridiculously high bets, and ruthless enough to develop a plan to kill the blacksmith and have a patsy ready to take the fall.'

'Would he have needed medical experience for the injection, or could he have just jabbed the needle into the skin?'

Trust Dolores to come up with a question they hadn't considered. Underneath all her glamour and artistic sensibility, Dolores possessed a warm heart and a remarkable amount of common sense.

'Marie should be able to tell us that,' he said. 'That would point towards the doctor.'

'Or anyone with nursing experience, like an orderly. Didn't the ambulance drivers pitch in in emergencies too?'

'Possible. Many ambulance drivers were conchies, though.'

'If they were willing to save soldiers driving an ambulance, they surely would have been willing to save them with an injection.' They sat at a table overlooking the stage from the upstairs balcony. Dolores watched with satisfaction as the band set up their instruments, before she turned her attention to the case in hand.

'True,' Jack said, 'but most people wouldn't hire a conchie.'

'They might not have known.' Dolores smoothed her dress over her knees. 'He'd have to be an immigrant. You and Simon and all the rest of you volunteered. There was no need to plead you're a conchie.'

'But none of them would hurt a soul.' The conscientious objectors Jack had met during the war had possessed no less courage than the men in the trenches. Driving an ambulance when shells and mortars exploded right around you or bearing stretchers was too often an undertaking as lethal as carrying a gun. The only difference was that the conchies refused to bear arms.

Jack had heard of cases in England where the men were sent to prison for their refusal to join the army and having a conchie in the family was seen as a stain on your honour. Emigration would solve that problem, but still – 'I can't see these men change their conviction to such an extent,' he said.

Dolores gave him a quick sisterly peck. 'I'll need to get changed for my show,' she said as she rubbed a lipstick smear off his cheek. 'Let me know if there is anything I can do.'

'I will.'

She swayed away, in unconscious sync with the tune played downstairs.

A happy, if unrelated, thought struck him. Dolores had been able to talk about the war without flinching. That was new. Her husband and Jack's best friend, Simon Grant, had been killed shortly before the armistice, making Dolores a widow at seventeen. Maybe he should sound out Phil about his intentions, as soon as he'd sorted out the present mess.

They arrived at the racecourse during a training session. The faint smell of horse sweat and manure infiltrated the building, thanks to the open windows.

Jack inhaled deeply. 'This takes me back to my childhood,' he said. 'Horse-drawn carriages and buses and hardly a car on the street.'

'It was all swell in spring and autumn,' Uncle Sal said. 'But I remember a summer so hot, the horses dropped dead in their tracks, and the bluebottles were buzzing around in huge clouds. Don't get me wrong, I love horses, but in their right place.' He fanned himself.

They'd whittled down their list to six names. Three trainers had horses running on the same days that Alfie, Miss Molly and Lady Lilly started. Two turf club presidents had attended a meeting in Adelaide the day before the murder. They'd added them at the last minute, after Marie noticed a short mention of the meeting in an article.

The last name belonged to the doctor. One of Bluey's contacts had mentioned another O'Leary who worked at Fremont. While it was entirely possible there existed no connection between them, the likelihood was strong the two men were related.

They'd excluded the stable hands. Although this group could walk anywhere between stables and lodgings with impunity, they stayed at one racecourse. It would also be hard to hide the fact that one of them had come into money when they were at the bottom of the pay-list.

Of special interest to them was the trainer of Alfie and Miss Molly. The racing programmes had given his name as A. Young, with no further information.

The one name Frances's list had added was that of the vet so recently replaced by Rob, and his new address in Mount Barker. It had struck them as curious that a horse vet would relocate to an area renowned for its vineyards, where he couldn't expect too many patients.

Bluey and Marie would take a geek at him later that day. The Top Note had a reputation for its high-class cellar, and people liked to chat everywhere.

Marie had confirmed that the tranquiliser would have been injected intravenously, but she'd also seconded Dolores' opinion that there were enough people around with the necessary skills.

Rob would be officially charged any day now. They needed to work fast to save him.

rances tapped on Mr Henry's door before she poked her head into the office. 'Good morning.'

Mr Henry motioned her inside with one hand, while he punched in numbers on his machine with the other hand.

The typist rattled away at his desk with renewed alacrity.

'I won't bother you too long today,' she said. 'I've only the guest list left to do.'

She inserted the paper and typed away, consulting her open notebook every now and then.

'That reminds me, Mr Sullivan asked me to add your staff to our list of invitations. If you'd let me know who to write down?' Frances gave them the brisk, efficient smile that suited Miss Whitford. 'It's a plus one, of course.'

'We're invited?' The typist gaped at her in rapt

delight.

'That is very kind,' Mr Henry said. 'Very generous indeed.'

'It's the least we can do to repay you for putting up with us.' Frances limbered up her fingers. 'The names, please?'

She stepped down the stairs with a sense of accomplishment. On top of having gained considerable goodwill, she'd also found out that both Mr Lucca and Mr Dunne were unmarried and thus much more likely to be charmed by Dolores, if they needed a distraction.

Marie nestled her head against her husband's shoulder. A drive into the verdant Adelaide Hills was a rare treat for them, and she promised herself she'd make the most of it. They were sure to find a tea shop in Mount Barker, where she planned on having lunch with a side-order of gossip.

The Rover purred with the regularity of a satisfied cat, a light breeze ruffled Bluey's hair and made Marie hold on to her hat for a second. If this had been a carefree outing, she'd have been perfectly happy. Her Hobart aunt had promised to ring her up without delay with any morsel of information she could find. Marie's telegram and subsequent phone call via the post office had thrown her into a flurry of excitement.

'You alright, love?' Bluey asked. 'It's not like you to be

so quiet.'

'I'm thinking how lucky we are.' She breathed in a lungful of sweet-smelling air, scented by the clover that covered vast tracts of land. Farmers used it to feed their livestock. The German settlers had also introduced vines to the region, together with town names that smacked of their native country.

Occasionally they saw a farmhouse in the distance, or farmers tending to their sheep. Mostly though, it was Marie and Bluey, all alone on the open road. Well, apart from the small terrier she'd borrowed from their neighbours.

Hobbes knew her well enough to be on his best behaviour, in the knowledge he'd be rewarded with a juicy bone later. 'It's pretty here,' she said. 'Peaceful. It's hard to imagine we're still so close to the city.'

'It's different alright,' he said. 'Makes you wonder why a bloke would give up the city for this.'

'It's not exactly the back of beyond,' Marie said. A Ford came towards them, and the grizzled driver lifted his hand in a salute. He chewed on a toothpick as he passed them. On the back of the Ford, three sheep were squeezed together. A kangaroo hopped across the street, ten feet ahead of them.

Mount Barker reminded Marie of her childhood. Tidy houses lined the few streets, and everything had a sleepy air. A small church, a schoolhouse and a shop with baskets full of fruit and vegetables outside seemed to be the most important buildings.

Bluey stopped the car.

Marie took Hobbes's leash and stepped out onto the wide pavement. This town was almost too clean and quiet, she thought. The school children would be in class, but shouldn't there be toddlers playing in their gardens, women tending to heir vegetable beds and old people chatting on the doorstep? In Adelaide, there'd be a few beggars too, or Raggedy Ann's playing an instrument in the hope of being given a few pennies.

'Come back, you old duffer,' a woman yelled, breaking the spell. A stocky man in a grease-stained shirt and frayed pants streaked past, cramming bacon into his mouth.

Marie giggled.

Hobbes flared his nostrils, no doubt enticed by the bacon aroma.

'Come on, mate,' Bluey said to the dog.

Marie nodded towards the shop where a woman swatted at flies. 'Why don't you two take a little stroll?'

A tinkling bell announced her arrival. Inside, shelves were half empty, but the wares were placed so evenly it was barely noticeable. It was a rare shopkeeper these days who could afford to order huge stocks without taking a gamble.

Jack insisted on the Top Note paying its invoices in full, within a few days of receipt, thus endearing himself to his suppliers. Not many others had the means to do the same or were inclined to part with their money before they absolutely had to.

Marie picked up a loaf of bread, cheese and two tomatoes and took them to the counter.

The woman put the fly swatter away and gave her a tooth-gapped smile.

'Hot today,' Marie said. 'I thought it's cooler outside the city.'

'You're from the big smoke?' Was there a note of longing in that voice?

Marie handed her a pound note. 'We're on our way to the vineyards. Do you have any local vintners?'

'A few. But most don't sell by the bottle.'

'It's not for us. It's for the Top Note, down in Adelaide.'

'The nightclub?' The women's eyes grew round.

'Yeah. We're supposed to bring home a few samples.' Marie sighed. 'That is, if we can do our job. Do you have a veterinarian in town? Our dog has been sick twice today. That's never happened before, and I'm starting to worry.'

The woman handed Marie her change. 'There's old Doc Mitchell, a mile or two further down the road.'

'Has he been here long?'

'Longer than most folks. You couldn't budge him with a pitchfork.'

'It must be tough to deal with such a large area when you're getting on.' Marie clucked her tongue.

'He's fit as a fiddle, is Doc Mitchell. And he's hired a helper. Youngish man, but I'd see the old doctor if I were you.'

'Thank you. We will.'

Marie caught up with Bluey and the dog sitting the shade under a white cedar. She sat down next to them, breaking off chunks off bread and cheese for Bluey.

Hobbes whined.

'Sorry, mate.' She patted his head. 'You'll get your treats later.'

They found the surgery with ease. A white shingle outside a grey weatherboard house with a wide porch announced Dr. vet. H. Mitchell. Nothing indicated the addition of another vet.

Marie, with the dog by her side, lifted the snake-shaped knocker and banged it against the door. Heavy footfall inside announced a person.

An elderly man opened the door five inches wide and blinked at her. His head barely came up to Marie's nose. 'The doc's not in,' he said without a preamble.

Marie laid her face into sorrowful lines. 'Will he be long? It's my little dog. The baby won't even sleep without Hobbes in the room.'

'Is there a problem?' A baritone voice rumbled through the hallway.

'I told the sheila the doctor's not in.' The elderly man shut the door. An instant later, it was flung wide open, and a man in his early forties with an easy smile and manners to match beckoned Marie and Hobbes inside the hall.

'Please do forgive our housekeeper. He's had a bad night with his rheumatism.' Judging by the dark looks the housekeeper shot at the traitor, he also suffered from jealousy.

'I'm Eddie Gant, the new associate.' He bared his gleaming white teeth at her in an ingratiating smile. 'What's the matter with this little fellow?'

Marie carried Hobbes into a well-scrubbed surgery faintly reeking of carbolic soap. Hobbes pressed his body against her chest. She stroked him as she lowered him onto the table. 'He's been sick. Once at home, once in the car.'

Eddie peered into Hobbes's ears, mouth, and checked heartbeat and abdomen with his stethoscope.

Hobbes gave Marie a hurt look.

'He seems fine now,' Eddie said. 'Did he eat anything unusual?'

Marie gave this considerable thought as she scanned the vet. His shoes were hand-sewn, but worn, and his clothes also showed slight signs of wear. A man with a decent amount of money, but not too flush.

'He stole a piece of left-over chocolate from my birthday.' Marie stroked Hobbes's nose. 'You look familiar. Have I seen you in the city? Somehow I connect you with horses.'

'I've been to a lot of places.' Eddie studiously averted her gaze. 'Chocolate would do it. The stuff can poison a dog.'

She clapped her hand over her mouth in feigned horror. 'I didn't know that.'

'There's an easy remedy. Eat them yourself.'

'I will.' She snapped her fingers. 'The racecourse. Am I right?'

'Fond of betting?'

'Fond of the horses. You don't see many around anymore unless you live on a farm. What brought you here? It seems a bit remote.'

'You don't like the countryside?'

'It's beautiful, but I think I'd miss the city after a spell.' She opened her purse. 'What do I owe you?'

Marie carried Hobbes to the car, fussing over him in case anyone watched her.

'How did it go?' Bluey handed her a bottle of water before he started the engine.

'Swell,' she said. 'Nice man, who wouldn't talk about his former work at all.'

'Maybe he left under a cloud.'

'Then this old cove here wouldn't have taken him on.' She shook her head. 'He left because he felt something was off.'

'You don't think he'd tell you anything?'

She pulled a face. 'He liked me, but the answer's no. A dead blacksmith would spook anyone.'

'Fair enough.' Bluey swerved to avoid another kangaroo. 'And now?'

'Now we visit a vineyard or two.'

## CHAPTER TWENTY

Frances straightened her skirt. It had bunched up a little over the padding because she'd wiggled around on the car seat, agonising over her next steps.

She rapped on the office door. To her surprise, Mr Lucca opened it. He gave her a quizzical look.

'May I use your phone after lunch?' She flashed him a brief smile. 'Otherwise I'd have to go all the way back to town, and there's still so much to do.'

'Today?'

'We need to organise flowers, press coverage.' She ran out of steam. 'I don't need to bother you with the details, but of course we want this ball to go down in the history of Adelaide and Morphettville racecourse for all the right reasons.'

'I am busy today.' He pondered this.

'No worries,' Frances said. 'I can take care of my phone calls while you're on your lunch break.'

He cast a quick glance back, at the locked drawers.

'Or maybe your boss could keep me company if you'd rather I'd not be alone in your office.' She attempted a light laughter, as if to emphasise the silliness of that idea.

'He's out of town today.' Mr Lucca paused. 'I haven't seen Miss Barden around. Is she alright?'

'You know her?'

He smoothed his already smooth hair. 'I've seen her at the Top Note.' His voice held the light tremble Frances had grown accustomed to in connection with Dolores.

She made a quick decision. 'It's possible that she'll drop by later. I'm sure she'd love you to say hello.'

Mr Lucca's eyes lit up. 'I'll let you know when it's convenient for you to use the telephone.'

Frances found Tony standing upright on a high step ladder, with Pauline circling it like a demented mother hen.

'What are you doing?' Frances craned her neck. Tony tapped a metal hook with an eyelet into the ceiling and threaded a thin rope through it.

'Careful,' Pauline said. 'You're wobbling.'

He wasn't, though, except in Pauline's eyes.

Frances led her away. 'Is that for the swing chair?'

'I've offered to test it for Miss Barden.' Pauline bit her knuckle. 'Only I'm not sure anymore.'

'If Tony builds it, it'll be good as gold,' Frances said. She wasn't too sure about the mechanics herself, with a crank handle to lower and raise the chair.

'Where is everyone?'

'Bluey and Marie aren't back yet. Mr Jack is in his office.' Pauline lowered her voice. 'He's waiting for news from Tassie. Uncle Sal is -'

'Still here.' He pushed a laden kitchen trolley with tea, cake and sandwiches. 'The cook was kind enough to give me a hand.' He winked at Frances. 'Nice lady. She's been here for years.'

'Can Tony run back and fetch Dolores? We might need her.' Frances grinned.

'If you don't think Mr Jack would mind me driving the big car?' Tony grabbed the rope and swung himself around. The eyelet turned freely without the hook moving so much as a hair's breadth.

Uncle Sal waved his objection off. 'If you bring back that chair of yours, we could see it in action. That'd be a beaut to watch.'

Mr Lucca popped in while Tony and Dolores were still on the way. Frances clutched her handbag with her notes and her lock-picks as she followed him. 'We'll reimburse you for our calls,' she said.

'Your rent should cover that,' he said. 'Unless you intend to phone up the whole country.'

'Marvellous how easy it is nowadays, with all these phones. It must make your life so much easier, and for breeders and trainers it must be a god-send.'

'True,' he said.

'I've always wondered if people receive a tip when there's a promising horse coming up for auction or if they just go and decide on the spot.'

'Both, I assume. There are folks who can tell after a few minutes if a horse is going to be a racer. That's rare though.' He gave her an interested look. 'Is Mr Sullivan branching out?'

'I hope not. It's such a risky business. I was simply curious.'

Frances placed her notebook, a pad and a pen next to the telephone.

'I'd be happy to show him around,' Mr Lucca said.

'I'm sure he'd appreciate that.' She picked up the receiver and dialled the number of the exchange. Using Miss Whitford's voice came easy by now. The last thing she needed was one of her colleagues at the exchange switchboard to recognise her.

Two phone calls to florists later, Frances tiptoed to the door and glanced outside. The passage lay empty. She wished she could sprinkle sand or anything else that crunched under feet to warn her, but it would be too conspicuous.

She put on gloves, fished out the skeleton keys and

slid them into Mr Lucca's drawer. Her stomach lurched as she pulled out a ledger. She forced herself to breathe evenly as she opened it, careful not to tear the pages. Here, in a precise copperplate hand, were all the business expenses listed. She turned page after page as quickly as she could, before she returned the ledger and took out the one underneath. Surely, she wouldn't be alone much longer.

Frances said a silent prayer as she finally found the entries she was looking for, including the list of staff and travelling jockeys for the races just before the old vet left, the first race of the year that had another painted horse running, and the fatal one in which the blacksmith had recognised the painted horse.

She copied the few names that hadn't been on Mr Henry's list.

Next should follow the list of horses, including owners and trainers. Frances flipped the page. Nothing. But that couldn't be, according to the content list.

If authorities asked to see them, Mr Dunne or Mr Lucca needed to hand those lists over. They had to exist.

Frances's head turned towards the small safe she'd only noticed today. It was made of steel and bolted to the floor. Her heart hammered against her chest. It was one thing to open a drawer and snoop around in ledgers and another to break into a safe that probably held all the takings on a race day.

No. It was too risky. But on the other hand, Rob's life was at stake.

Her hand trembled as she rifled through the ledgers again. One page was loosely inserted, entering Alfie into a race. And it was signed by Mrs Cowper and the trainer, whose name Frances couldn't decipher at first glance.

She still held it in her hand when she heard faint noises. She slipped the paper into her shirt, closed the ledger and fumbled to lock the drawer as fast as she could. She'd only turned her skeleton-key halfway when the door flung open and Mr Lucca entered.

The blood drained from her face as she searched for an explanation.

'Hello there.'

Mr Lucca's head swivelled around as if drawn by a magnet. In the doorway stood Dolores, draped oh so casually against the frame and giving Mr Lucca a full dose of her high wattage smile.

She held out her hand. 'I'm Dolores Barden, and I want to tell you how grateful I am to allow us to perform in these magnificent halls.'

Mr Lucca bent over Dolores' hand for a kiss. 'The pleasure is all mine, I assure you.'

'In this case, may I ask you for a huge favour? I'd love to see the horses up close.'

His gaze travelled down her legs, to her strappy shoes. 'I'm not sure your pretty heels are suitable.'

Frances willed herself invisible while she locked the drawer completely and slipped the skeleton keys back into her bag. She gave Dolores a tiny signal.

Dolores beamed at Mr Lucca. 'How right you are. If I bring proper shoes tomorrow, maybe?'

'I'd be honoured,' he said, gazing at her in open admiration.

Frances picked up her bag and notebook. 'I'm all done here,' she said. 'Thank you, Mr Lucca.'

He snapped back into the present. 'In this case, let me take you ladies back to your stage.'

Frances trotted behind the pair. She marvelled at the ease with which Dolores charmed men. Otherwise she'd have been deep in trouble.

Mr Lucca kissed Dolores' hand again before he returned to his own duties.

Dolores closed the door, a half-smile on her lips.

'You were wonderful,' Frances said. 'Your timing was perfect.'

'I'd been on the lookout,' Dolores said. 'He's a perfect pet, isn't he?'

'Who is?' Pauline asked, with a wink at Tony.

'Mr Lucca.' Dolores eyes took on a shrewd look. 'I wonder how many hands he's kissed.'

'Glib?' Tony asked. His original shyness towards Dolores had been melted faster than the snow on the Adelaide Hills on a spring day.

'Smooth. Attractive, too.' Dolores shrugged. 'It would be a pity if he ended up replacing Rob in prison. One can never have too many admirers.'

~

They returned to the Top Note in high spirits. Tony was happy because the swing seat found Dolores' full appreciation, Pauline was happy because her new costume awaited, expertly sequinned by her mother, and Frances felt it in her bones that they were close to finding out who was the mastermind behind cheating at races and murdering the blacksmith.

The mood of her waiting conspirators proved her right. Uncle Sal swept Frances into his arms and waltzed with her into the office.

Marie's eyes sparkled, and Bluey beamed like a child at Christmas. Jack leant against a wall, an unreadable expression on his face.

Uncle Sal prompted Frances to take a seat.

'What have you found out?' she asked. 'Did you locate the vet?'

'Child's play,' Marie said. 'Rather a nice man, who doesn't want folks to know he had anything to do with the races.'

'Oh.' Frances's hopes took a dent.

'Chin up. If he'd just departed because he'd had a bellyful, or fancied a change, he'd have mentioned it.' Marie made a dramatic pause until Jack's ominous signal towards the wall clock made her hurry up. 'He won't talk, but that as good as proves that there was something that made him bolt. Which means we'll need a close gander at the last race days before he quit.'

'And look for familiar names or unexpected wins,' Frances said.

'Too right. And there's more.' Jack pushed a folded telegram over to her.

She opened it and read, *"Mrs Cowper used to own a couple of racehorses before the war. A cove named Young has a training stable about ten miles from Launceston. He's said to have only two stable boys, and visitors aren't welcome."*

Frances paused. 'So, I guess he could know everything about the old lady from her racing days.'

'He might even have worked for her,' Jack said. 'Marie's aunt phoned up to mention that her old manager was a bloke nicknamed Old Pom.'

He was too far away from Frances to hug. Instead, she jumped up and hugged Uncle Sal.

'Wait till you hear the next bit,' Marie said. 'Old lady Cowper has been widowed forever, and her son died in the Second Boer War. The daughter passed away a few years ago, but she's said to have married an Italian.'

'Did your auntie have a name?' Frances didn't want to get her hopes up too high, but it couldn't be a coincidence. Even with all the immigrant communities, non-British people still stood out.

'No. It was too long ago, and she got married in Melbourne or Brisbane. But her son, if she had one, would be in his thirties or younger.'

Mr Lucca's face flashed up in Frances's mind. His eyes, as he saw Dolores, and the awe with which he'd kissed her hand. Still, criminals could be charming. She knew that from the talkies. 'Raffles' in particular, held a place in her heart, with Ronald Colman as the gentleman jewel thief, who only returned to the game to save a friend with gambling debts. Maybe that had been Mr Lucca's downfall too, a fondness for cards or betting on the nags. But his motives didn't matter, not really. And anyone framing her brother for murder was beyond redemption.

The stolen document made a crinkling noise as she moved. 'Close your eyes, everyone,' she said.

Jack gave her an astonished look, before he obeyed with the rest.

She fished the paper out of her shirt. 'Now you may open your eyes again.'

Jack gave a surprised whistle as he took up the document. 'Where did you get that?'

'The drawer in the office. I couldn't read the name of the trainer in a hurry.'

'It is a particularly illegible scrawl.' Jack held it up to the lamp. 'Parrett, or Barrett, maybe. At least the address is clear enough. There can't be many horse trainers in Charleston.'

'Never heard of the place,' Uncle Sal said.

'It's got to do with flour mills, doesn't it?' Marie asked. 'Something in connection with the man who set up all those steam mills in the last century.' They all gaped at her. 'There was a brochure in the vet's surgery,' she said. 'I only caught a few sentences.' Marie looked around. 'We never know what matters in the end, right?'

'True.' Jack furrowed his brows. 'If we had more time

to spare, I'd say you and Bluey tale another trip to the countryside.'

Frances mouth went dry. Only a few more days, and they'd lose their access to Morphettville. Meanwhile, Rob must be close to despair.

Uncle Sal appeared to notice her sudden fear. He stroked her hand. 'No need for that,' he said. 'Bluey and I'll drop into the tavern for another round or two. I'll eat my hat if my new bookie friends don't have the good oil on any horse trainer within a couple hundred miles. That is, if you can spare Bluey for a few hours.'

'Please, Jack?' Frances swallowed. 'I wish I could go along, but they wouldn't talk to me.'

'Have you no faith in me?' Uncle Sal twinkled at her. 'I've never dropped my part yet. Which means, we should better rehearse our real act now, if I'm to toddle off with Bluey later.'

Jack nodded.

'Anything more for me?' Marie asked.

'Could you phone up your aunt and ask for more information on Old Pom? And see if she can remember when Mrs Cowper's daughter married her Italian. We might find the wedding notice in the papers.'

Marie wrinkled her nose doubtfully. 'If she got the city right. But I'll try.'

Frances's mind whizzed away as she stepped into her

roller skates. She was grateful for the distraction. Twirling Uncle Sal on his chair at exactly the right speed took all her concentration. Pauline waved at her as she stepped into her straps. This could all be heavenly, if only Rob were safe.

'One, two, three,' Uncle Sal sang out. She grasped the chair and set off, listening only to the rhythm of Uncle Sal's counting. During the performance, one of the musicians would instead bang a timpani drum.

The first knife sliced through the air, sticking to the frame one inch from Pauline's left shoulder.

# CHAPTER TWENTY-ONE

*U*ncle Sal shuffled into the tavern. Five o'clock, a full hour left for legal boozing. He hoped he'd calculated correctly, and his new mates would call in for a snifter or two.

Again, Bluey lounged in a corner, with a pint of Coopers in front of him and engrossed in the racing forms in the newspaper. No-one gave him a second glance.

Uncle Sal hid a grin as he spied one of the bookies at the bar. He took the stool next to him. 'Join me in a tipple?'

For a moment, the bookie was taken aback, before he recognised Uncle Sal in his persona as the loquacious Bernie. 'Don't mind if I do,' he said. 'Mine's a West End.'

Uncle Sal signalled the bartender. 'Make that two pints.'

He waited until the glasses stood on the counter. 'The nags treating you right?'

'Can't complain,' the bookie said. 'Mind, it's tough times for anyone.'

'Don't I just know it.' Uncle Sal swigged his beer. 'But with two days' pay in my pocket, and a couple days promised, my daughter let me off the leash.'

'Women,' the bookie said with a grimace. 'They can't stop nagging a man.'

'It's in their blood,' agreed Uncle Sal, silently adding that in his experience the naggers had a good reason, and he'd met a darn sight more whining from men than from the ladies. He leant closer and lowered his voice in a confidential tone. 'A little bird whispered something in my ear, a tip straight from the horse's mouth.'

'You falling for that?'

'Not me,' Uncle Sal said. 'Unless – that little bird said, this here trainer has a golden hand with the fillies.' He slid the bookie a quick glance. 'Not that I'd bet on them here at Morphettville. But there's a race meeting coming up in Ballarat, where a mate of mine is going.'

'Ballarat, eh? Not a bad course, but nothing beats us here. Not even Fremont.'

'I'll drink to that.' Uncle Sal raised is glass. 'The trainer's name is Parrett or Barrett, down Charleston way.'

'Bartlett?' The bookie scratched his head. 'Bit of an odd duck, that one, but yeah, his horses seem to do alright lately.'

'Odd duck?'

'Keeps himself to himself and won't have anyone watch him working with his racers. He's only got three or four going, from what I've heard. Not that I've met that man.'

'So, a little flutter on his charges wouldn't be crazy?'

'Not crazier than all the others.' The bookie finished his beer and gazed longingly at the empty glass.

'Another one?' Uncle Sal held up two fingers for the bartender.

'Two reclusive horse trainers.' Frances mused as she sat with Uncle Sal. They'd retired to the lounge as soon as they'd finished the omelette he'd insisted on whipping up. The wireless ran in the background, more out of habit than anything else.

'That can't be a coincidence,' Uncle Sal said. 'And if you think about it, it's perfect. You bring in one proven champion, fiddle with the papers, and out comes a novice who bags an unexpected win, while you've placed medium sized bets at a number of places. If that blacksmith hadn't recognised the hoof, they'd have been safe, and he'd still be alive.'

'They can't have placed the bets in person, could they? But if they'd phoned them in, how do you collect your wins?'

Uncle Sal broke into a wide grin. 'You're brilliant.

That's a fair enough question. That means Jack's old mates could have a chin-wag with their local bookies in the places where we're sure there was something crooked.'

'It all takes so long,' Frances said. 'I feel like we're treading in place.'

Uncle Sal gave her an affectionate squeeze. 'You worry too much. We're getting close enough, don't we? We've got the trainers, the link to Tasmania –'

'And not a shred of proof.'

'Not yet. But we will. And then it'll all come right as rain.'

Frances shivered despite the warmth of the evening. She hadn't told Uncle Sal how close she'd come to being caught picking the lock of the drawer. She hoped Dolores wouldn't mention it either. Jack and Uncle Sal didn't mind taking risks themselves. When it came to Frances, though, they became overprotective.

If only she hadn't overlooked anything. Tomorrow, Mr Dunne would be back, and sneaking into the office would be next to impossible, now she'd made use of her one pretext.

Jack watched the revellers with a practised smile on his lips. It was hard to imagine the poverty in the streets and the number of people relying on the susso to keep their children from starving. Here, at the Top Note, champagne flowed, and at the few dining tables, steak and pies were staples. Nothing went to waste though. Leftover food was taken home by staff members or handed over to the soup kitchens the next morning.

Jack wondered if their quarry had at one time graced these very halls. Maybe he was here right now, dressed in tails and dancing by, an expensive sheila in his arms. Considering how lucrative the racket with the painted horses must be, it was highly likely.

'White Jack Sullivan.' Someone smote him on the back.

'Councillor.' Jack shook a plump, manicured hand. The councillor had had the good fortune to marry into money, added refinement included.

'The missus is just freshening up,' the councillor said unprompted. 'And seeing you here all alone, I thought I'll pop over for a sec.' He broke off as Dolores entered the stage to thunderous applause. 'Now that is a woman,' he said.

'One in a million,' Jack agreed. He paused, wondering what the councillor wanted. Jack was known to support worthy causes, but he rarely received outright requests for favours.

'The thing is,' the councillor said, struggling to tear his gaze away from Dolores in her figure-hugging white dress, 'the missus tried to get hold of a few tickets for your big do at Morphettville and couldn't.' He made a face. 'You are popular, my friend.'

'Not me, Dolores Barden is. And then of course,

there's the good feeling that you're supporting out-of-work artists and orphans. Without the huge demand, we wouldn't have moved the ball to the racecourse.'

'You couldn't squeeze us in, could you?'

'Leave it to me. How many tickets shall I put you down for?'

The councillor silently counted on his fingers. 'Make it ten, there's a good chap.'

'Not a problem. You can sort out the payment before you go.'

Jack moved on, exchanging pleasantries while keeping a close eye on proceedings.

The Top Note had a reputation for clean, good fun, and he made sure it stayed that way. Intoxicated guests saw themselves sent home with their drivers or with a cabby, and drugs were a no.

He glanced at the stage. Dolores was in glowing form, but he detected a hint of sadness in her velvety voice. They needed to clear Rob for her sake too, before she missed Phil too much. Her detective boyfriend would attend the charity event, where he could easily mingle. Until then, there could be no open contact, for both his own career's sake, and for their investigation. Their crooks mustn't link them with police at all if they didn't want to spook them.

'Boss?' Bluey handed him a cold soft drink. 'Almost closing time.'

They had strict rules for weekdays. At one o'clock, the party was over. That also helped the cabbies who knew when to turn up for fares. Weekends were different, though, with the music playing until three. Female employees didn't work that late. At midnight, they left together, to be driven home.

Jack rolled his aching shoulders. 'Do we have enough people to take care of the show and keep the Top Note open for our regulars?'

'She'll be apples. And if not, Marie has enough people who'd drop everything to pitch in.'

'Makes you wonder though, how large a crew it takes for our little spot of bother.'

'I was thinking that too.'

Rob lay on his lumpy mattress, wondering about the same thing. The first shock and fear had passed, and now a strange detachment had gripped him. He could see his predicament, yet from a removed perspective, as if this body wasn't really his and none of this existed outside his mind. It wasn't denial, or fatalism, simply a nice level of disconnect allowing him to stay sane. He'd experienced a similar state once before, when he had flu and his mid floated on a cloud of serenity while the fever raged through his body.

He'd treat this like an academic puzzle. How many people did it take not just to make a switch possible, but profitable? And where would they need to be based?

It all had to start with the trainer, who knew which

horse he could "paint" and pass off as an unexperienced nag only starting out on the racecourses. The owner didn't necessarily have to be in on this.

The trainer might then be travelling with the horse, but would he risk openly betting high on the nag? Maybe with one bookie, Rob decided. But one bet wouldn't be enough by far to make it all worthwhile. He'd lay a wager that every single bookie operating on the course was stung. That took either a number of people in each city, or one adept at changing his appearance. Someone like Uncle Sal.

Rob drifted off, oblivious to the heavy snores from the other cells.

Jack insisted on a proper breakfast for everyone. Or, more likely, Marie had suggested it, Frances thought as they tucked in. It gave them a chance to make sure everyone was coping, too, without being obvious.

Only Dolores was missing. She never rose early, and Jack would brief her on their way to the racecourse later in the day.

Jack gave Frances a quick grin as she helped herself to more bacon. For a few days, she'd hardly eaten, until he reminded her that it helped nobody if she made herself ill. This meant she could also truthfully tell her mother over the phone that everything was right as rain.

Mum knew better than to ask direct questions, aware

as they all were of the possibilities of an operator listening in, but she worried.

Marie seemed fidgety, unlike her ordinary unflappable self.

Frances swallowed the last mouthful. Everyone else was finished too. Frances stacked her plate on top of Uncle Sal's and moved around the table to help clear it.

Marie waved her off. 'Someone else can take care of that later. We've got better things to do.'

Frances followed her to the office.

Pauline and Tony left reluctantly. They were expected at Dolores', even if it meant missing out on possible developments.

The office was crowded enough without them. Frances sat on Uncle Sal's armrest, while Jack gave his chair behind the desk up to Marie and leant with Bluey against the wall.

The clock struck ten. The phone rang. Marie picked up. Her eyes sparkled. 'Thank you, operator,' she said, which meant she must have prearranged the call. 'My auntie,' she mouthed.

Frances leant forward.

Marie shoved pen and paper towards her.

'Good morning,' she said into the receiver. 'Yes, we're all quite well.' She listened for a moment. Her face lit up. 'You do have more news for us?'

Marie signalled Frances to write down what she said. 'The Italian worked at a restaurant in Melbourne,' she said. 'Something with – right, a foreign name.'

She nodded, although her aunt couldn't possibly see her.

'He was either a waiter, or a delivery driver and chauffeur. Yes, horse-drawn carriages, of course I remember.'

Horses! Frances pinched herself.

'His mother-in-law wasn't too impressed. She had no time for pretty young foreigners.'

Frances wrote as fast as she could.

'What about Old Pom? I see.' Marie grinned. 'You're a brick, Auntie. Wait.'

She looked up. 'Do we have any more questions?'

Frances and Jack exchanged a glance. Frances shook her head.

'Ask her to be available again tomorrow again,' Jack said. 'In case something crops up.'

Marie followed his instructions. 'Bless her,' she said as she ended the call. 'She was getting worried about the costs for us.'

Frances checked her notes. 'You said something about Old Pom.'

'Oh yeah. My auntie remembers him as a handsome fella, who popped up about forty years ago. Always dapper and cheerful and a dab hand with the horses.' Marie grinned at her stolid husband. 'Almost as handsome as my Bluey.'

'And?' Jack prompted her.

'It all went smoothly with him and Mrs Cowper until shortly before the war, when she caught him fiddling the till, so to speak. Forging invoices, altering feed bills and other stuff. He was a bit too fond of the cards, it seems. Pity. She kicked him out on his seat pants and withdrew from racing.'

'Before the war,' Frances said. 'He's probably too old now to be involved in this racket.'

Uncle Sal gave her a hurt look. 'Us older folk can do lots of things.'

She pecked him on the cheek. 'True.'

He ruffled her hair.

'How can we identify our elusive Italian?'

'There can't have been that many restaurants with foreign names,' Uncle Sal said. 'And he probably had an accent. Tuscan, I'd say.'

They all gaped at him.

'The name, Lucca. It's a town. Birthplace of Puccini.' Uncle Sal looked around. 'The composer. Honestly, sometimes I wonder about this world.'

'Yes, yes,' Frances said. 'So, you think he took on a false name?'

'Much more likely that the immigration officer or the shipping office bungled it up on his ticket. It took me an hour to make them add the final letter to my name. If he was from Lucca, they could have used that.'

'But who would be able to help us more than thirty years later?'

'Never underestimate the veterans' network,' Jack said. 'Bluey, you'll take care of that while I keep the Top Note ticking over.'

Frances experienced a stab of disappointment, and guilt. This investigation proved costly and time-consuming enough for Jack, and still she'd hoped to have him around when they went to Morphettville.

'If only I could get into that office again,' she said out loud.

'At the racecourse? Why?' Jack asked.

'It's probably nothing, but I was wondering about the safe. Wouldn't they have books for keeping track of their income? Like, where they had their manipulated bets placed and for how much? Or payment to accomplices?'

'No way. It's too dangerous,' Jack said. 'If we have enough to go on, we'll take this to our friends in the police force. I don't think your brother would appreciate a family reunion behind bars.'

# CHAPTER TWENTY-TWO

The rehearsals were in full swing as Bluey dropped Frances, or rather Miss Whitford, and Uncle Sal off. Dolores sat in her swing chair, radiant with joy, as Tony raised and lowered it and she used her legs to give to added momentum.

Pauline stood transfixed, beaming at her sweetheart and her much admired employer. She had been unable to resist dressing in her costume, in the hope Uncle Sal had recovered enough to practice his number with her.

She fluttered her lashes at Frances, who by now had grown used to her wig and the padded costume. 'I was thinking, Miss Whitford, maybe you could fill in for Signorina Francesca?'

Frances hesitated. The last thing she wanted was to draw attention to herself, which on roller skates was inevitable. On the other hand, it might establish them as two different women. 'My pleasure,' she said. 'That is, if

Doctor O'Leary declares Mr Bernardo well recovered enough.'

They'd taken the precaution to strap Uncle Sal's ankle again. He pretended to groan as she took his arm.

Outside, three boys led prancing horses around the track. The sun glistened on their shiny coats, and Frances could see the muscles on their necks.

A dappled white flicked her tail over her back, to rid herself of flies and mosquitoes.

Uncle Sal stopped. 'Now that's a sight to behold.'

'They are beauts,' Frances agreed. 'But –'

He grimaced. 'No rest for us. I know.'

They waited outside the surgery while the doctor treated yet another jockey who left with a mutinous look on his face.

Doctor O'Leary shook his head as he ushered Uncle Sal and Frances in. 'Young idiot,' he said. 'They all are. Banged up like billy-oh, and too stupid to see they can't get in the saddle with three cracked ribs. One more tumble, and they'll pierce his lung.'

'That bad?' Uncle Sal whistled surprised. 'He didn't look all that crook.'

'Painkillers and sheer grit,' the doctor said. 'Now, what can I do for you?'

Uncle Sal let Frances remove the bandage.

'I can't in all good conscience allow Mr Bernardo to rehearse without your medical opinion,' she said in her primmest secretary voice.

'As bad as a jockey, is he?' The doctor guffawed.

Frances thought she detected a hint of alcohol on his breath.

'Not quite, but we take our responsibilities seriously.'

Dr O'Leary probed Uncle Sal's ankle. 'Bend it to the left,' he said. 'Excellent. Now to the right, please.' He patted Uncle Sal on the back. 'Clean bill of health for you. I'd leave the ankle strapped up, to give it more support, if you can, but you're good to go.'

A knock on a backdoor Frances hadn't noticed before interrupted him.

'Oi, Doctor.'

'Come in,' the doctor called out.

A gnarled man sidled in. In his hands he carried a large, brown bag. 'You forgot your work boots,' he said in a gruff voice.

The doctor peered at his dress shoes. 'I did indeed. How's that possible?'

'Always in a rush, that's why. Doesn't take more than a butcher's hook to make sure you've got everything, but no.' A pair of sly eyes flickered to Frances. 'Although the ladies do like a toff.'

'Off with you.' The doctor motioned good-naturedly towards the door, and the man shuffled out.

'My factotum,' he said. 'You must excuse his cockney manners.'

A cockney. That meant London, and a Pom. Frances had trouble hiding her excitement.

'Been in the country long?' Uncle Sal asked.

'You mean because he hasn't succumbed to Aussie

slang? Forty years is nothing to a man born within hearing of the Bow Bells.'

'That's nice of him, running all the way here to bring you your boots.'

The doctor laughed. 'He just wanted to save himself the trouble of cleaning my good shoes. And it's a pleasant walk if you cut across the racecourse. My house backs onto it.'

Uncle Sal slipped into his shoe. 'Thanks a lot, doctor.'

They shook hands. 'I hope not to see you again, at least not professionally.'

'Which reminds me,' Frances said. 'You're of course invited to our charity concert. How many tickets shall I put you down for?'

'That's kind of you,' he said. 'Just the one will do me.'

'No worries.' Frances gave him a courteous smile. One ticket meant he lived alone, and if his house backed onto the racecourse, he or his factotum could easily have gained access to Rob's chamber.

She remembered the sly glance and easy familiarity of the Cockney, which was pronounced even for Australia.

## CHAPTER TWENTY-THREE

*A*rthur Dowling hopped off the train, his swag on his back. The din of Melbourne washed over him. People were bustling every which way on the station, in a constant hurry. He had to step lively, to avoid bumping into a joker who couldn't be bothered to pay attention to his way.

Arthur heaved a sigh of relief as he made it outside. How people could live like this, was beyond him. They were worse than ants in an anthill. Now, a smallish place like Ballarat, where you could be friendly with folks and still go undisturbed about your business, was more to his taste.

He looked up his piece of paper with an address supplied by Bluey. A boarding house only one stop away from Flinders Street, run by another veteran and his wife.

He found it easy enough. Not a bad place, he decided

as he took in the freshly painted porch and the well-kept trim. It did him good to see old soldiers falling on their feet.

A man with a slight limp opened the door as soon as Arthur swung the brass knocker. He gave him an appraising look. 'You Bluey's mate?'

'Aye. The name's Arthur.'

Arthur followed the man inside, into a scrupulously clean hallway and to a room at the back.

'Bathroom's outside,' the man said. 'It's got a tub and everything.'

A woman bustled into the room. 'Welcome to Melbourne,' she said. 'Tea's ready in the kitchen, if you'd like some refreshment.'

Arthur gratefully accepted a cuppa, and a thick slab of homemade cake. The kitchen was a little too pink and frilly with its dainty curtains and ruffled tablecloth, but it suited Paula Johnson with her bright eyes and rosy cheeks. Her husband Kev relaxed slightly as they sat together.

'Bluey said you're staying as long as you need to.' Kev waited for an answer.

'I hope that's alright with you.'

'Sure.' Paula laughed. 'Any customer's welcome if they behave themselves, but friends of friends are always special. What can we do to help?'

Arthur hesitated, but Bluey wouldn't have sent him here if the Johnsons weren't trustworthy.

'I'm looking for a man who worked at a fancy foreign restaurant about thirty years ago.'

'That's a tall order.' Kev pinched the bridge of his nose. 'Shouldn't be too hard to find the restaurant. There's still not too much foreign chow around. But a bloke who used to give them a hand back then? Good luck with that, mate.'

'He was Italian,' Arthur said. 'That might be something people remember. They would in Ballarat. And he married an Australian girl by the name of Cowper.'

Paula pushed her lips in and out, as she pondered this. 'Didn't you come home on the ship with an Italian soldier, Kev? The one who wouldn't shut up about proper coffee making?'

Her husband broke into a lopsided grin. 'Good old Gio,' he said. 'He's still around, and you know how people are. Sticking together with their own folks.'

'Can you point me in his direction?' If Arthur was lucky, he could be done in a day or two. Not that he minded staying with the Johnsons, but Bluey had said his task was urgent.

'If you can stick around for a few hours, I'll take you to the hotel where the old soldiers usually hang out.' Kev noticed his wife's sudden frown. 'I'm not drinking, love, you know that. But you can't blame a man for having a pint or two.'

'That would be swell,' Arthur said. 'Where shall we meet?'

They arranged a time, and Arthur excused himself. The bathroom was tacked on to the back of the house, with a separate entrance. A rustling noise from inside the drain suggested that a critter or two had found a home there, but everything else was as sweet as could be, with a tub, a sink and mirror, and a toilet.

His own lodgings in Ballarat didn't stretch that far, although a dunny and zinc bath served him and his fellow lodgers well enough. The Johnsons seemed to do well enough for themselves.

Arthur stepped out onto the streets in his best suit. The jacket hung a little loose on his frame, and the pants were starting to fray. Yet he'd still count as well-dressed, considering the sorry state most folks were in. From what he could see, you were either a flash cove in Melbourne or reduced to wearing rags. There were not many people in between.

He held his hat in his hands as he entered the office of *"The Argus"* on La Trobe Street.

The smart receptionist gave him a perfunctory smile as he asked to see the archives.He breathed a little easier when she told him to follow her, without asking any more questions. All he had to do was sign in, and off they went. Her heels clacked on the floor as she led him to a large room and handed him over to a dried-out old man. The walls were lined with shelves holding large, bound volumes.

The old man coughed, the kind of polite cough not

caused by a sore throat but by a desire for the other party to state their business.

'I'm looking for a marriage notice,' Arthur said.

'Yes?'

'But I only know the approximate date.'

'Indeed.'

Arthur grew hot, despite the coolness of the room. He moistened his parched lips.

'And the groom was Italian.'

The old man tut-tutted. 'That's all?'

Arthur shuffled his feet. 'It would have been around the late 1890s.'

'You can have a look, although with this little information, there's not much hope.'

The old man hefted two large volumes with an ease that astounded Arthur and placed them carefully on a table. Two chairs sat ready for visitors. 'Let me know when you're through.'

Arthur's eyes smarted from scanning page after page. Luckily, *"The Argus"* kept family notices and obituaries in the same spot every day. He took great care to turn the pages without tearing or creasing them. The old man watched him like a wedge-tailed eagle.

Arthur's neck developed a crick as he sat, searching through year after year. The tiny print hurt his eyes. He glanced at his watch, to make sure he didn't miss his appointment with Kev as something caught his eyes. A wedding announcement, for Easter 1896, between a Miss Susan Cowper of Hobart, Tasmania and a Mr

Giuseppe Rossi, formerly of Tuscany, Italy, and now Melbourne.

Arthur grinned to himself. He took out an old envelope and a pencil and carefully copied the words.

'Thank you,' he said to the old man. 'You've been most helpful.'

The man surprised him with a smile. 'Anything else, you'll find me here.'

Arthur bounced onto the street, only now allowing himself to be intimidated by the Argus building. He'd never been anywhere that elegant or huge before, and the idea that eight floors could just be there for one newspaper was unfathomable. And yet the staff hadn't been snobby at all about an ill-educated man like him, who had come close to licking his pencil before he wrote. Even better, he'd actually done it. He had a name for Bluey and Captain Jack.

Kev waited outside a shabby hotel. Paint peeled off its weatherboard and the patch of garden had more bare patches than grass. Despite these signs of neglect, the windows shone.

Inside, a group of men aged beyond their years sat around a table at the back. They all looked as if they could do with a square meal. Arthur felt a stab of remorse for all the hours he'd spent pitying himself. Why, with people like Captain Jack and Bluey to fall back on, and hardly any hungry days, he should count himself lucky.

Kev knocked on the table. 'Fellas,' he said. 'Mind if

we sit down?' The men willingly made space for them. Arthur slipped Kev a pound note. He didn't want to make it too obvious he was here to buy information.

'Beer alright with you?' Kev asked around. Seven heads nodded.

'Make it Victoria Bitter,' one man who had two fingers missing on left hand said.

Kev strolled to the bar.

'You're new,' the man with the missing fingers said to Arthur.

'I'm just passing through,' Arthur said.

'Looking for work? You won't find any.'

Arthur thanked Bluey for giving him a cover story. Otherwise he'd have been in a spot. 'I'm here to do a mate a favour,' he said. 'He's in a bad way and you know how it is. A cove gets to thinking about his family, and the people he should have been in touch with. It's what I did when that German bullet hit me.'

One of the men shuddered. 'I still hear the mortars whistle.'

The man next to Arthur whispered, 'He was a sapper. Got buried for two days and nights when the tunnel caved in.'

Kev came back, carrying a tray full of pints.

'So, how can we help?' the man next to Arthur asked.

'My mate is a bit hazy, but he thinks as he might have an aunt and uncle here in Melbourne. An Italian. Used to drive horse-drawn carriages.'

Arthur took a long pull from his bitter.

The other men looked at a man with gleaming black hair and dark eyes. 'You know anything, Gio?'

'Did he have himself a local wife?' Gio asked.

'Too right he did.' Arthur leant forward.

Gio pulled a face. 'Could have been old man Rossi.'

Arthur's heart beat faster.

'Do you have any idea where I can find him?'

'Melbourne General cemetery,' Gio said. 'He's been there since 1918. The Spanish flu got him. Sorry, mate.'

'At least I can tell my friend that much.' Arthur took another swig. 'Did they have any children?'

'One son, I think. They didn't mingle too much.'

'Ah well. Family can be tricky. Next round's on me.'

# CHAPTER TWENTY-FOUR

*B*luey hung up the phone and grinned at Marie, Jack, Frances and Uncle Sal. 'Spit it out before you burst,' Marie said.

'We've got the good oil from Melbourne,' Bluey said. 'Old Arthur has come up with the Italian.'

Jack clapped him on the shoulder. 'About time. Is it Lucca?'

Bluey's chipper mood deflated. 'Name's Rossi. But Arthur said as he was originally from some place called Tus, Tus-something-or-other. What Uncle Sal mentioned.'

'Tuscany?'

'That's the one.'

Frances looked at Uncle Sal. 'You said the officials bungled up foreign names.'

'Or the son changed it himself, to hide something.'

Jack smiled at Frances in a way that made her heart skip a beat.

'We've got Mr Lucca, then,' she said. 'Ad we might even have his helper. I can't really see Mr Lucca bash in a head with a horseshoe.'

'And his accomplice would be?'

Frances grinned. Despite everything, this was her moment, and she intended to enjoy it. 'Old Pom. I think he works for Dr O'Leary, which gives him access to the racecourse buildings, he knows his way around, and he should have enough knowledge of medicine.'

Uncle Sal chuckled. 'He's definitely a proper Cockney, and his age is right too.'

Marie gave her husband a loud kiss on the cheek. 'What are we waiting for? Let's get the police to take over.'

'We still have no proof,' Jack said.

'What could there be to find?'

'Papers,' Jack said. 'Even a crooked businessman will keep track of his pennies. We only have one set of accounts, because we're honest, but I bet you anything, there is a complete paper trail.'

'The safe,' Frances said. 'There's a safe in the office. I could open it.'

'No.' Uncle Sal and Jack spoke in unison.

'If anyone does it, it will be me.' Uncle Sal's face took on its stubborn look. 'If we get caught, I'm an old man. I've got nothing much to lose.'

'Nobody will get caught,' Jack said. 'You know why?

Because nobody will touch that safe until we've come up with a cracking plan. Pun intended.' He touched Frances's hand.

'But you too believe there's something in there?'

'If it's at the racecourse, yes. And I can't imagine a fraudster and possible murderer would carry around incriminating material any further than he needs.'

Frances rose. 'Then all we need is a plan, and we're all set.' A hopeful smile played on her lips.

Jack nodded. 'The sooner we have an inspiration, the better.'

Frances helped Uncle Sal to his feet. 'We should go home. Unless we're needed here?'

'You should go, too, Marie,' Jack said. 'If you make sure your troops are in place when we need them for the show, you and your aunt have done more than enough.'

'I'll drive them,' Bluey said.

'Thanks.'

Marie had a smug little smile on her face as she declined the passenger seat and squeezed herself in with Uncle Sal and Frances at the back.

'Captain Jack is getting overly cautious,' she said in a low voice.

Bluey heard her, nevertheless. 'That's how he's kept us all alive during the war. You listen to him.'

'We do,' Frances said. 'As if we'd ever ignore his

advice.' A tiny voice inside her head whispered that listening wasn't the same as obeying. She understood why Jack tried to steer her away from any danger, but if it helped Rob, she wouldn't allow herself to be stopped by anyone. Not even Jack.

Marie winked at her. Frances settled into her seat. Together they could not fail.


Frances handed Uncle Sal a mug of hot tea. She'd scrub the kitchen after they they'd had a chat. The whole house wasn't up to her mother's standards lately, but Frances didn't care. She'd blithely ignore the state of the kitchen too, with its food stains on stove and floor and a light grease film everywhere if she could trust Uncle Sal not to don an apron and clean every nook and cranny on his knees.

They settled into their usual spots on the sofa.

Uncle Sal slurped the hot tea, startling Frances. His manners normally tended to be impeccable.

He twinkled as he caught her look. 'Just getting into character, love. In case good ol' Bernard is needed again to chat up the bookies.'

Frances lifted her pinkie as she sipped her tea in her most refined manner. 'Is this right for Signorina Francesca?'

He kissed his fingertips. 'Perfect. Now, tell me about that safe.'

Frances thought back. 'It's a bit under hip-high and

'this wide.' She spread her arms slightly to indicate the size.

'What kind of lock?'

She didn't understand.

'One with a key, or a combination lock with rings and numbers?'

'A key.'

He blew out his breath, much relieved. 'Do you remember what it looked like?'

She closed her eyes and tried to picture it. 'Yes.'

Uncle Sal hurried away, to return with the locks she'd practiced on what seemed like ages ago.

She lifted them each carefully. Only two resembled the lock they were after, both almost ten inches in diameter and with a heavy pin tumbler mechanism.

Uncle Sal grimaced. 'Yale locks. They take a little longer to crack, with their pin tumblers. I should be able to do it in under two minutes though. We just need enough of a distraction.'

'But you have no reason to be in the office at all,' Frances said. She angled for her purse with the skeleton keys. 'I'm the only one wo has got an excuse.'

'You, or Jack.' Uncle Sal switched on the wireless. 'Let's see if a little music helps us figure out a way.'

Frances sneaked along the hallway to Dolores' apartment. If for some reason Jack was still home instead of at the Top Note, she didn't want him to hear her.

She knocked softly. After an interminable wait, Pauline opened the door.

She gaped at Frances who put a warning finger over her lips and jerked her head towards Jack's apartment.

Pauline pulled her inside.

'Who is it?' Dolores asked.

'It's Frances.' Pauline followed her friend.

'Frances, darling.' Dolores raised a languid hand. She rested on a day bed. Her face was covered in a thick white cream, and cucumber slices lay on her eyes. She took them off. 'What brings you here?'

Pauline handed Dolores a damp flannel, to pat away the cream.

'I need to ask you a favour,' Frances said. 'One you can't tell Jack about.'

Dolores shot upright. 'How intriguing.'

Frances counted the hours until Dolores would join them at the racecourse. Their rehearsals were nearly finished. A few run-throughs of Dolores' act, and of Uncle Sal's daring number, and they were ready. With only three days to go until their big event, Miss Whitford would soon have to disappear, to make way for Signorina Francesca.

Dolores breathed in, trailed by a faint scent of

heavenly perfume and an awed Pauline. She gave Frances a tiny signal.

The conductor rushed over to greet her at the door. He was painfully shy, with his Adam's apple bobbing up and down as he bent over Dolores' hand. His tailcoat had seen better days, if it was his in the first place. But he and his band were top notch, Uncle Sal had told Frances, and his judgment with regards to music could always be trusted.

'Shall we do the songs in order, or what do you prefer?' Dolores asked.

The conductor's eyes widened. 'Whatever you want.'

'In this case, let's get the tricky bit over with.'

Dolores motioned to Tony to lower the swing seat. The conductor lifted her into it, although she could easily have climbed on herself. A bewitching smile played around her lips.

Frances in her secretary role watched as the chair with Dolores in it was raised again. She slipped out of the room.

She knocked on the office door.

'Yes?'

Instead of Mr Lucca, his boss stood in front of her, in his shirtsleeves. A pile of newspapers and documents sat on his desk.

'I was looking for Mr Lucca,' she said, primly.

'Is it important? He's still in town.'

Frances masked her disappointment. 'Mis Barden just wanted to invite him to watch her rehearsal.'

'He should drop in within the hour,' Mr Dunne said as he flashed her a wide smile. 'I'm sure he'll be only too happy to have a geek.'

Frances slunk away, back to the rehearsals, where Marie put refreshments. Dolores was mid-song, and the chair was lowered so slowly that, with the lights strategically placed, the audience would first see her sparkly, golden shoes, spectacular legs and then the rest of her.

Frances joined Marie who tasted a sandwich.

'I asked my friend Andie to arrange for a food parcel to reach your brother,' Marie said unprompted. 'We made it big enough to share with the wardens, or any cell mates.'

'I did worry,' Frances said. 'I can't imagine there's lots to eat in prison, but if the other guys think Rob is being treated special, it could be bad for him.'

'A few more days,' Marie said. Her smile was meant to be reassuring, although it didn't hide the doubt in her eyes.

Frances shifted her attention to Dolores. How was it possible to convey so much heartbreak with her music and yet be so uplifting?

She broke into applause as the last note petered out. Dolores blew her a kiss and hopped of the swing chair.

Frances indicated to wait half an hour.

Dolores dazzled the conductor with a blinding smile. 'Smoke-oh and then the rest of the songs?'

Frances spied Mr Lucca as his car pulled up behind the main building. She watched him climb the stairs to the first floor. What was he doing there?

Dolores had gone through her songs twice as Frances saw the assistant manager finally stroll towards the office.

She unwrapped a pair of brogues and held them up for Dolores to see.

The singer fanned herself. 'You gentlemen are amazing, but I need a break. Give me an hour, will you?'

She slipped her arm through Frances's.

'Wait,' Frances said. She took a thin coat out of a bag.

'Coo-ee,' Dolores trilled as they knocked on the office door.

'Miss Barden.' Mr Lucca opened. He gazed at her in open admiration.

'I hope I'm not disturbing you.'

'No, not at all.'

'You see, I've wrangled an hour's break, and you did say you'd show me the horses if I wear suitable shoes.' She dangled the brogues.

'Absolutely. You mean, now?' He shot Mr Dunne, who was busy reading, a quick glance.

Dolores wrinkled her nose in a manner that reminded Frances of Claudette Colbert in the pictures. 'I guess I can't lure your boss away too?'

'I wish I could tear myself away,' Mr Dunne said. 'Next time.'

Frances helped Dolores into the coat which covered up the dress perfectly. Dolores tied the belt tightly around her waist.

'Allow me.' Mr Lucca held out the brogues. Frances took away Dolores' stage shoes. 'You can leave us, Miss Whitford,' Dolores said.

Frances gave her a small bow, unsure if that fit in with her role or was a bit too subservient. Not that it really mattered. Mr Lucca was much too smitten with Dolores to pay Frances any attention, and Mr Dunne had returned to his reading.

She decided to visit the kitchen. If she left the door open, she might be able to hear anyone leaving the office. Five minutes, that was all she was asking for.

To her chagrin, nothing happened. The cook and her helper accepted her offer to peel vegetables while she hung around. Frances suspected their easy acceptance of her had a lot to do with the fact that Jack had promised to cover their wages while the catering team took over. Getting paid for nothing wasn't something they'd experience often.

'Do you always have the same jockeys?' she asked, to show interest.

'Pretty much,' the cook said. 'Much too expensive to have them traipsing up and down the country. They tend to stick to a few places.'

'So, only the horses and trainers travel?'

'And the bosses. They all know each other.'

That would have made it easier for Mr Lucca, to also figure out who to entrust with placing the bets.

Dolores' happy chatter alerted Frances that her chance had passed. Maybe that was for the best though.

'When do people here go home at night?' she asked. 'Do they keep office hours? Mr Sullivan is keen not to make anyone staying late on our account.'

The cook shrugged. 'If you don't count the jockeys and the vet, it's lights out at six unless it's a race day.'

'Excellent.' Frances put down the peeling knife and washed her hand over the sink. 'We'll try to be as considerate as possible.'

She almost forgot herself and skipped along the hallway. After six, they should get away with a little light burglary.

# CHAPTER TWENTY-FIVE

*D*olores buzzed with happiness. She sniffed her hand. 'I'd almost forgotten how good it feels to stroke a horse's nose.'

'That was kind of Mr Lucca,' Frances said.

Dolores fluttered her lashes. 'He is a darling. Everyone here is so kind to us. We should really think of something.' She gazed at the band. 'I'd say, once more, and then we're done here?' An impish gleam in her eyes made Frances hopeful.

Dolores insisted on keeping quiet until they were almost home. She tapped on Bluey's shoulder. 'Is there a florist in the Arcade?'

'There might,' he said. 'There's one around the corner. They used to supply your lilies.'

'Then please take us there.'

Dolores declined any help and insisted on Frances and Bluey waiting in the car.

'What do you think she's doing?' Frances stared out of the window.

'No idea. Anything that makes Miss Dolores this happy is good, I'm sure.'

Dolores ambled back to the car with a handsome young man in tow. He had his arms full, with a potted orange Kangaroo Paw in full bloom.

Bluey hurried out of the car and opened the back door. The young man carefully eased the plant inside, making sure it stayed undamaged.

'That's spiffing.' Dolores pressed a coin on him. His face took on a deep pink tinge.

Dolores took the passenger seat, now the space next to Frances was occupied by the plant.

'To the Top Note,' she said with a mischievous grin.

Bluey switched the engine on.

Dolores declined to say a word until they were all assembled in the main room. The plant, which reached up to Frances waist, took up too much room to fit in the already cramped office.

She gestured towards it. 'What do you say, Jack, darling?'

'It's a beaut. Where do you want to put it? On stage?'

Her velvety laughter filled the room as she nudged Frances into the centre. 'It's a prop alright. I thought it will give Frances a nice little cover for her big moment.'

Frances and Jack both stared at her.

'People tell me things,' Dolores said. 'I've seen the safe, and I bet you're itching to discover what's inside.'

'Fair enough,' Jack said. 'But then you should also know that I'm not letting Frances take any risk.'

'Which is why I've purchased this beautiful plant to say thank-you for showing me around the stables.'

Frances caught on. 'We're taking it there tonight.' Excitement surged in her veins.

Dolores dangled her slim wrist. 'I've already lost my bracelet in the corner by the window as I changed my shoes. As you can imagine, I'm distraught and will have you search for it. Which is when you also take my little gift along. If the guards catch us, they won't think twice about it.'

Jack gave her a pained look. 'Finding a plant in the morning is a give-away that we've illegally entered an office which is kept locked.'

'We could put it in front of the safe,' Frances said. 'It's big enough to hide it and block any view of the safe from the door. Once I've picked the lock –'

Uncle Sal coughed. 'I'll do it. My risk is no bigger than yours and I have more experience in this stuff.'

Jack opened his mouth. Frances clapped a hand on his lips. 'The offices are deserted at six. We take the plant, and if anyone sees us, the office was unlocked, and we just searched for the bracelet and delivered the gift. Otherwise we'll take the potted plant away with us again. There is hardly any risk.'

'I have to be back here by nine,' Jack said.

Frances was surprised he'd given in so easily. She

gave him a delighted kiss on the cheek. 'It'll only take minutes.'

'It should be dark around 7.30 tonight,' Jack said. 'If we arrive at dusk, it'll look less suspicious.'

'It's enough if Bluey and I go,' Uncle Sal said.

'I'll do it. Rob is my brother.' Frances jutted out her chin.

'And you're my responsibility.' Uncle Sal glowered at her.

'I'm in this as well,' Dolores said.

Frances's jaw dropped.

'You need me,' the singer said. 'If we're in trouble, you need a star frantic to retrieve her bracelet, and if that's not enough, I'll faint in a spectacular manner.' She reached out for Jack. 'I promise I won't be in the way.'

'Anyone else?' Jack harrumphed. 'We might as well hire a coach to the racecourse.'

Frances's stomach knotted in anxiety as they rolled onto the racecourse grounds. For the last fifty yards, Bluey had switched off the engine.

Despite her words she realised how likely it was that something would go wrong. Jack would be fine, of course, and so would Bluey. She worried about Dolores, who'd never had to move stealthily before, and who attracted attention with every step. Then there was Uncle

Sal. Despite his acting and lock-picking skills, he had a gammy ankle. One misstep, which could happen only too easily should they have to run, and they were done for.

The main building lay in darkness.

'We have to be quiet,' Jack said before they left the car. 'Try to act normal, though. If you look as if everything's fine, most people won't bother to think what we're doing here.'

He went first, followed by Frances and Dolores and then Uncle Sal. Bluey, with the plant, brought up the rear.

Jack, wearing silk gloves like Uncle Sal, unlocked the entrance with the key Mr Dunne had given them. He shone a torch at the floor, with the beam low enough to be invisible from the outside and yet giving off enough light for them not to stumble.

'We can't all go in the office,' he said. His eyes pleaded with Frances.

She relented. 'Dolores and I will keep ourselves ready in our rehearsal room. If we hear or see anyone, we'll imitate a kookaburra.'

Jack gave her a quick hug. 'Bluey, you'll stand guard by the back door.'

Frances and Dolores sneaked to their places. The moonlight cast a sickly glow through the half open curtain and cast Dolores' shape in sharp relief. Frances pulled Dolores into the darkness. She heard her heart beating. Dolores felt for her hand. Together they stood with bated breath.

~

Jack stood frozen, every fibre of his being alert. He listened to the sounds of the building, the scrabbling of tiny feet outside, the sharp cracks as the heat of the day dissipated. He'd held sentry like this back in the war, day after day and night after night, an experience he'd never wanted to repeat.

Yet here he was again, fighting for a man's life while trying to keep his troops safe. Uncle Sal, who concentrated on opening the door without making a sound, and who so clearly was willing to sacrifice himself should they trip up. Dolores, whose generosity and selflessness he'd never doubted, and who nevertheless was so ill-equipped for clandestine acts. And then there was Frances, his sweet, stubborn girl, who would bravely face hell for someone she cared about.

Of all of them, only Bluey gave him no cause to worry. He knew too well how unflappable his big, silent second-in-command was, even if all hope seemed lost.

Uncle Sal opened the door inch by inch and slipped through.

Jack took the potted plant which Bluey had left with him and arranged it so Uncle Sal could go to work on the safe unseen.

Jack glanced around, the beam of the torch directed towards the safe lock. Uncle Sal didn't need much light, but if he relied only on touch, he would leave tell-tale scratches in the metal.

Jack slowed down his breathing. Uncle Sal might be able to hear the pins tumble rather than feel it in his sensitive fingers.

The old man nodded to himself, as if in a silent conversation.

One minute had gone. Jack wondered how Frances and Dolores were doing.

Uncle Sal moved his head slowly and grinned at Jack as he slowly, so slowly, opened the safe. It made a tiny squeak, and Uncle Sal stopped for an instant before he went on.

Jack shone the torch into the opening. Two ledgers sat at odd angles. Jack silently cursed. It was easy enough to put neatly aligned books back into their rightful place, but if they moved these, anyone paying proper attention would notice. Especially a criminal, who was willing to kill to protect himself.

Uncle Sal stretched out his hand.

'Don't,' Jack whispered.

'There's something else.' Uncle Sal peered closer. Jack moved the torch. At the back of the safe, well-hidden behind a steel money box, with only a few millimetres of a white cap to be seen, stood a small bottle.

'I'll lift it,' Jack said. 'There's another one.' He held

the first bottle into the light. 'Horse tranquiliser,' he said as he put it back.

Uncle Sal's voice sounded hoarse. 'And the other one?'

Jack lifted that, too. 'Digitalin.'

# CHAPTER TWENTY-SIX

*U*ncle Sal locked the safe again. In the hallway, Jack whistled softly as a sign for Bluey, before they picked up the girls.

Frances didn't say a word. He smiled at her, to let her know they'd succeeded.

The potted plant rode back in the boot.

Jack waited until they were on the main road. 'We need a chin-wag with Phil,' he said. 'Can you arrange a meeting in your apartment, Dolores?'

'I'm due on stage in an hour.' She creased her forehead in fierce concentration.

'Tomorrow morning will do. Ask him to take the fire stairs at the back.'

'It's almost over, isn't it?' Frances rested her head against Uncle Sal's shoulder, suddenly too tired to stay upright.

'Too right it is, kiddo,' Jack said. 'Just a few more

things to be done, and Rob will be free.'

To her dismay, Frances felt moisture well up in her eyes, and a fat tear rolled down her cheek. Uncle Sal handed her a tissue. 'Don't cry.'

'I won't. I'm simply relieved.'

Dolores crumbled her toast. Jack put his hand on top of hers. She'd called him over at what was for her an unusually early hour. He'd expected to see Phil with her, but that was the problem. She hadn't reached him, and his new landlady said he'd left with an overnight bag in his hand.

'It'll be fine,' Jack said, to calm her down. 'He'll come to our show, won't he?'

'He'd better.' Dolores lips wobbled. 'I could call the police station, to make sure.'

'Good idea.'

She reached for the telephone.

Jack excused himself and went into Dolores' shiny kitchen. She'd lately taken to cooking, as displayed by the egg-caked frying pan and dirty bowls. Jack put them to soak. Their housekeeper would take care of them later.

He heard Dolores ring off and strolled back.

Dolores frowned. 'He's not working today, or tomorrow.'

'Did it sound true or like an excuse?' Phil had come

236

to Adelaide after his undercover work in Melbourne had made his life as a police detective too dangerous.

I don't know. I asked the sergeant to give Phil a message to call on me at home.'

'That's alright then.'

'If Phil has gone to ground, what do we do?' Frances asked.

'Rally our other troops.' Marie exchanged a quick glance with Jack. 'I'm sure Phil will pop up when we need him most, but he isn't our only friend in the force.'

'He's the only one who wouldn't ask how the incriminating bottles came to our attention,' Jack said. 'Unless you want to involve Sergeant Miller.'

'He's a sensible man,' Marie said. 'His wife can be trusted to tell him what he needs to know.'

'In which case we still need to set a trap, so he can be on the lookout. We need our man to be caught red-handed.' Jack rubbed his smooth chin.

'Why would Mr Lucca keep the digitalin and tranquiliser?' Frances had been puzzling over that question.

'I can think of two reasons. The first is, that's it's not easy to rid yourself of evidence without anyone seeing you or finding it. Doesn't matter if you throw them into the Torrens, someone will see you. With a dustbin, the homeless might search through them.'

'And the second reason?' Uncle Sal asked.

Jack set his mouth in a grim line. 'As long as Rob isn't convicted, something could always go wrong, and he'd need another scapegoat to frame.'

'Or to murder.' Frances swallowed hard.

'Yes,' Jack said. 'That too.'

Bluey took only his wife, Frances, Pauline and Uncle Sal to the racecourse. The knife-throwing number was the last one that needed rehearsing.

Frances's hands shook on the way. What if Mr Henry came across her, or worse, Mr Lucca and Mr Dunne? Pauline had done her best to make her unrecognisable, and the blonde wig should also help. Yet she was apprehensive.

She kept her gaze lowered as they walked in. Faint noises from upstairs signalled Mr Henry's presence, and she thought she heard low voices from the office. Pots and pans clattered in the kitchen.

Marie quickly stroked her arm as she went off to finalise the catering arrangements. Flowers and trays with goodies for the large refrigerator would arrive the next morning, and she'd be busy decorating then with a few assistants.

Frances strapped on her roller skates. She fought hard to focus on being Signorina Francesca and forget about the murderer and the content of the safe.

Tony arrived, out of breath. He cradled a portable gramophone in his arms and sat it on a table.

In a bag he carried two recordings, or rather, two copies of the same music, in case one broke.

He checked the frame he'd built for the act and tugged as hard as he could on the wrist and ankle straps that would hold his fiancée.

Pauline twirled around in her sparkling costume, her bright smile rivalling with the crystal chandelier. Although she knew why they were at Morphettville, Jack and Frances had agreed it was wiser not to tell her too much about the firm suspicion pointing at the racecourse people. Pauline was prone to flights of fancy, and Tony too might give the game away if he thought his sweetheart was in danger.

Pauline snapped her fingers in front of Frances's face. 'Hey there.'

Frances broke her musings. 'Sorry. Ready whenever you are.'

She skated over to the frame and helped Pauline step into the holds.

Uncle Sal sat on his wheeled chair and lifted his head. Just a few movements, and he'd turned from an elderly gentleman into a commanding presence.

Frances clasped the back of the chair.

Uncle Sal gave Tony a regal nod.

Tony lowered the gramophone needle, and soft music filled the room.

'Now,' Uncle Sal said. Frances sprang into action,

counting the beat in her head. One, two, three, four ... All her senses were heightened as she anticipated Uncle Sal's every sharp move. Nothing existed except for the rhythm, the movement and the odd sensation of

having left her old personality behind.

'Enough,' Uncle Sal said. Frances dug in her heel to stop herself and the chair.

Pauline squealed with delight as Frances helped her out of the straps. 'That was brilliant.'

She flew into Tony's arms. 'How did I look?'

'Like a star.' They gazed into each other's eyes.

'Your smile slipped for a moment,' Uncle Sal said.

'It did?' Pauline's face fell.

'Only for a second,' Uncle Sal said. 'Think of the applause. That'll help.'

'You all looked fabulous to me,' Marie said from the door.

Frances hadn't even registered it opening.

Pauline's face lit up again. 'Good-oh.' She snuggled into Tony's arms.

'Are you done here? We need to set to it if we want this place to dazzle the crowd in two days.'

Frances turned to Uncle Sal. This was his call. 'Sure,' he said. 'I'm good, and my girls are too.'

They filed out of the room.

'Hello?' Frances spun around as she heard Mr Dunne. He barely glanced at her. 'Isn't Miss Whitford here today?'

Marie sighed. 'Her mother's been taken ill. She had to go home for a few days.'

'That's a shame.' He pondered. 'Could I entrust you with something instead?'

'Sure,' Marie said. Frances relaxed.

Marie followed Mr Dunne back to the office. She waited by the door as he neatly folded a letter, put it in an envelope and sealed it.

He glanced at the floor. 'That's odd.' He picked up something small and orange.

Marie cursed silently. A petal from the Kangaroo's Paw. It smelled strongly, too. Or, rather – she grinned. 'Is it possible that Miss Barden was here?'

'Yesterday.'

Marie took the petal and the envelope from him. 'Bless her, she loves orange flowers.'

'I still don't see the connection.'

'She adores to wear a flower pinned to her dress. The petal must have fallen off when she changed her shoes.'

Mr Dunne relaxed. 'That would explain it.'

'Will that be all?' Marie gave him a carefree smile. 'In that case, I'll see you later.'

'He had no idea who I am,' Frances said as they piled into the car, with Tony as chauffeur.

'I told you so.' Pauline pouted. 'As if anyone could see through your disguise. It's my best work ever.'

241

'It is.' Frances could have hugged her friend. In the confinement of the back seat, she had to settle for a big grin instead.

'What happens now?' Tony asked.

'You and me and Pauline will get our decorations out and start decking the halls,' Marie said promptly. 'And Uncle Sal and Frances will stay out of the way. The less she is seen, the smaller the danger that anyone will recognise her, and he can keep her calm.'

'You've worked miracles,' Frances said. 'But you know how Jack can be.'

Pauline rolled her eyes. 'Do I ever. Not that I can blame him. Tony would be the same, wouldn't you?'

Tony chuckled. 'You better believe it.'

The one thing that Frances and Marie didn't mention was the fact that they'd also be busy at the Top Note figuring out exactly how to trap Mr Lucca.

Jack tacked a clean blueprint of the ground floor layout to the wall.

Andie Miller had been instructed to alert her husband to the possibility of an incident which might require his assistance. They'd agreed it would be unwise to say too much, in case the Millers betrayed their interest.

Frances had timed how long it took from the ball room to the cloak room where they'd install Bluey, and to the office. The cloak room was in between the two. They'd put up a wooden barrier to make sure none of the party guests would venture beyond.

Unless Phil came to their aid, the starring role would have to go to Marie's friend Gillian, a former nurse and veteran member of an amateur dramatic society. She could be relied upon a convincing performance, and she could throw her voice while seemingly whispering.

Jack went through every aspect three times with Blue, Frances and Uncle Sal. Their plan wasn't watertight, or easy to rehearse when so many things depended on the party, but it was their best shot.

'Go home and get some rest,' he said to Frances after they'd finished their discussion. 'Ring up your mother and tell her everything will be fine.'

'Listen to the man.' Uncle Sal held out his hand. 'Come on, love. We'll see you tomorrow, Jack.'

To her surprise, Frances fell asleep on her bed and only woke up when Uncle Sal called her for their evening meal. He'd lit candles and opened a bottle of wine, a rare occasion. He raised his glass. 'To friends and to Rob.'

'To Rob,' she said. Her mother had sounded chipper enough on the phone, but then she had experience with a stiff upper lip. Rob's wife and the unborn baby kept well enough she'd said.

Frances hoped it was true. It would have been lovely to talk freely, but for the operator and for her sister-in-law's sake they had to skirt around the topic, relying on platitudes. Yet hearing her mother's voice had been oddly comforting.

~

Frances rose with a jolt as the sun shone through her curtains. She staggered downstairs where Uncle Sal had laid the breakfast table.

Frances rubbed her gritty eyes. Past ten already. 'Why didn't you wake me?' she asked as Uncle Sal poured her a cup of coffee.

'This will give you energy,' he said. 'You were all done in, love. And there's not a lot left for us to do.'

Frances had to admit he was right. They lingered over egg and bacon. 'Let's go for a walk,' she said when they had emptied their plates. Uncle Sal's skin had a pasty tone underneath his tan, and she probably looked like a ghost, too.

She barely recalled the last day they'd spent in the sunshine. She was either cooped up in the telephone exchange, which seemed like a lifetime ago, or lately at the Top Note or the racecourse.

'Elder Park?' he suggested. 'We could take a picnic. Maybe Jack can spare a few moments too.'

She shook her head. Jack had already given up every free hour and more. She dreaded to think how hard it must have been to keep the club running with everything else going on.

'Just you and me,' she said. 'Like we used to.'

They say by the river, feeding the ducks with breadcrumbs and wilted lettuce from their kitchen.

A light breeze rippled the water and the sun glinted like diamonds on the gentle waves. Frances leant back on her elbows. 'It's so peaceful.'

'Not a lot of that around lately,' he said.

His cheerful tone couldn't mask his pain. Poor Uncle Sal. What should have been a triumphant final return to his beloved stage had become a dangerous burden on all of them. Maybe they could perform their act at the Top Note once Rob was free and all this lay behind them.

She shot him a sideways glance, only to notice Uncle Sal watching her. They broke into laughter. Whatever happened, they'd have each other.

He rose and swung her to her feet. 'Your nose is taking on a rosy hue,' he said.

She clapped a hand over her face. Fashionable as sun tans were, she didn't want to end up with a red nose and forehead. They'd have to buy a cooling tonic on their way home.

Frances and Uncle Sal strolled arm in arm, both content in each other's company. Maybe she should miss her mother more, Frances thought with a stab of guilt. But as much as she loved her, at least for now, Uncle Sal was enough.

# CHAPTER TWENTY-SEVEN

'The big day.' Jack had assembled Bluey, Marie, Frances and Uncle Sal in the main room of the Top Note. There was something reassurance in his sleepy smile and his broad shoulders.

Frances sat there with a notepad on her lap. Any spur of the moment idea was welcome.

'Any news from Phil?' she asked.

'Not yet, but he'll be there tonight.'

'If he isn't, and we need Sergeant Miller to fall back on, how will we warn him?'

Jack motioned to Uncle Sal.

'It's going to be an almighty racket,' Uncle Sal said. 'About the same as the Top Note on New Year's Eve.'

'Which will make it impossible to send out a signal.' Frances had thought about this problem without coming up with a solution.

'Except that we've got orchestras and all the instruments under the sun.'

'As soon as we bait our trap, Tony will play a drum-roll. We'll make sure the bands are on break.' Uncle Sal beamed at Frances.

'That should work,' Marie said. 'I'll ask Andie to stick around with her husband, so he doesn't take a moonlight stroll at the wrong moment.'

The ball room was decked in flowers, the chandelier blazed, and black velvet curtains festooned with crystals muffled any sound from outside.

Marie's catering friends had outdone themselves with crustless sandwiches, sausage rolls, mini pies, pastries and fruit cut into flower shapes.

Dozens of covered trays waited in the kitchen, together with a tower of champagne glasses. Jack had pulled a few strings to receive a special liquor permit, because the charity show would also be attended by "bona fide travellers".

A dance troupe waited in the wings, to open the event.

Jack stood at the door, greeting guests together with Mr Dunne who welcomed them in his function as manager.

Frances bustled about in the dressing room while Pauline pinned up Dolores' hair with diamante clips.

'I should be having stage fright, not you,' Pauline teased her.

She could easily say that, Frances thought. Her friend had no idea how much depended on this night. Even Dolores had only been told that they needed Phil if he made an appearance at all.

'Stand still,' Dolores said. Frances stopped walking. She'd come to Morphettville ready dressed and wearing her wig. All she needed were her roller skates before her big act.

Dolores chucked her a lipstick tube. The metal felt cool in her hand, and smooth, despite the engraved flowers. 'Swipe it on. It'll calm your nerves.'

'Is that Elizabeth Arden?' Pauline's voice held an edge of awe.

'It's your colour, Frances.' Dolores gave her an appraising glance. 'My Chanel is too red for you.'

'Give it to me, and I'll paint your lips,' Pauline said.

Frances gave in, to please and to pass the crawling seconds. Also, Dolores swore by the calming powers of lipstick. If ever Frances needed those, it was now.

Marie called from outside. 'Fifteen minutes. We've got a full house.'

'Pout,' Pauline said to Frances, who dutifully pursed her lips.

"Don't forget the perfume.' Dolores sprayed herself from a cut-glass bottle. The scent of Chanel No 5 filled the room.

Frances declined. The ball room would reek of a

dozen different perfumes, and she didn't want to overload Uncle Sal's nose, or alert anyone in the wrong moment to her presence.

She squared her shoulders, took a deep breath and counted to twenty. They'd rehearsed as much as they could. Nothing more they could do now.

The orchestra played a soft drum roll.

Frances hurried towards the ball room, and Uncle Sal. Together they stood on the side-lines and watched Marie's old nurse friends glide through the crowd offering champagne.

They'd set up a bar, and a dining room area, at one end, as far from the hallway and office area as possible. They couldn't afford a single mistake.

A spotlight shone on Jack in his tuxedo. He smiled at the guests as he stepped up to the microphone.

'Welcome to this evening's entertainment,' he said. His voice was even, and there were none of the metallic noises and screeches that happened so easily with cheaper microphones. 'As you all know, this show will go towards helping those who are a lot less lucky than all of us assembled here. I have the great pleasure to not only promise you a few numbers no-one has ever seen before, but also the raffle of a great prize. The winner will spend a weekend at the Oriental Private Hotel in Glenelg, courtesy of the proprietors.'

Screams of excitement interrupted him. Frances could understand. An excursion to Glenelg Beach on the tram was the most fashionable and exciting trip she could imagine before meeting Jack, and only well-to do people could afford more than a few hours by the jetty.

'Tickets for one shilling each will be sold in the first interval. But now, ladies and gentlemen, let the music begin.'

The orchestra played the first song, and the ball was under way.

The dancers were still on stage for the opening act when it became clear that the evening would be a resounding success.

Dolores had yet to come out of her dressing room, but then she never made a public appearance before she was due on stage.

Jack navigated the room with the same ease he showed at the Top Note, all the while keeping a close watch on Mr Lucca who chatted animatedly with, of all people, shy old Mr Henry.

Mr Dunne with busy flirting with a golden-haired debutante, and Dr O'Leary stuck close to the bar.

'It's going swell,' Uncle Sal said as the dancers left the stage to ecstatic applause and the orchestra changed to a foxtrot.

Frances cast a longing glance at the dance floor. Jack was the most accomplished dancer imaginable, but they'd agreed to leave him to his host duties tonight. If people saw him with Signorina Francesca in his arms, someone might remember her as his girlfriend, plain Frances Palmer. Uncle Sal too couldn't risk hurting his ankle when so much depended on his mobility, despite his seated act.

'Ready?' Marie pressed a clipboard in her hand and hung a money-tin around her neck. She and Frances would sell the raffle tickets, with the buyers only having to put down their names.

'Already?' Frances frowned.

'After Dolores has worked her magic. But we need to be prepared.'

As if on cue, the lights were dimmed again, and a low, single drumbeat caught everyone's attention.

People cheered as Dolores came in sight on her swing seat. Frances marvelled at the effect. She'd had to climb on behind the curtain, let herself be raised high, and then lowered again while travelling at least twenty feet.

The spotlight caught her shining shoes, the silk stockings, and the draped, golden lamé dress.

Frances's breath caught in her throat. She'd never seen Dolores this stunning. Gasps from the audience confirmed that.

'Wow,' a voice behind her said.

Frances spun around. Phil winked at her. 'Later,' he whispered while he focussed on his girlfriend.

Frances clasped Uncle Sal's hand. With Phil on their side, they were safe.

Dolores held the audience in the palm on her manicured hands. For thirty minutes she sang, and

Frances could have sworn it couldn't have been longer than five minutes.

She saw Phil and Jack exchange a few words while she beamed at guests and the shillings poured in for the raffle tickets. The crowd squeezed happily together, and she had to move quickly to avoid being jostled. The heat of the room flushed her cheeks under her powder. A flash bulb in a corner announced a press photographer.

Frances giggled. She already knew which picture would make the papers. The photographer might snap away, but nothing could compete with Dolores on her swing seat.

'Frances.' Pauline waved at her.

'One moment,' she called out as Mr Dunne put his name down for three tickets.

She dashed into the dressing room and put down her clipboard, which now held a dozen sheets of paper with names, and the money-tin. She stepped into her roller skates.

Pauline's eyes were wide with excitement as she danced onto the stage and allowed Tony, who looked like a fashion plate in a cleverly altered old suit of Jack's, to help her into position.

Her smile shone brighter than ever as the audience clapped.

Frances pushed herself off and twirled before pushing Uncle Sal and his chair in place. She rolled five yards away.

Tony handed her the set of knives.

The guests fell silent.

The drums beat. Frances curtsied, Uncle Sal lifted a hand, and she threw the first knife over to him. He caught it by the handle, just like the second, third, and fourth.

Frances curtsied again, rolled over to Uncle Sal and counted the beat under her breath. They were at a forty-five-degree angle to Pauline as he threw the first knife. A woman screamed.

Frances faltered for a second, then found her rhythm again. The second knife whizzed through the air, then the third, and the fourth.

The applause made the floor sway. Uncle Sal rose and took a deep bow. Loud whistles greeted him. He held out his hand to Frances, and they bowed together.

Tony helped Pauline down and stepped out of the way. The spotlight moved away from Uncle Sal and onto Pauline, who for one brief moment, was celebrated like a star. She still stood there on stage, shining brightly, as Frances rolled into the dressing room.

She sat down to take off her roller skates as her gaze fell upon the clipboard, with the raffle ticket orders. There was something about Mr Dunne's signature. Michael Joseph Dunne, with a leftward slant.

The truth knocked her for six. She'd seen that particular handwriting, on the document she'd stolen from the office. Only then the signature had said, Josephine Cowper. Not Mr Lucca, but his boss had falsified the papers for the painted horses.

# CHAPTER TWENTY-EIGHT

*F*rances rushed out of the dressing room, only to catch Gillian stage-whispering her rehearsed lines in Mr Lucca's earshot. She said to a friend, 'This is between you and me, but my mate whose brother works at the prison, said they'll release that vet. The poor bastard's innocent of murder.'

Frances spun around. Mr Dunne leant against a wall and enjoyed a sandwich, too far away to hear anything.

She frantically searched for Phil and Jack. A warm hand touched her shoulder. She stifled a scream. 'Everything okay, kiddo?'

'We've got the wrong man,' she said into Jack's ear. 'Mr Dunne is the one.'

'Sure?'

'I've recognised the writing.'

Jack took her by the hand.

People clapped as she rolled past them, convinced this was part of the entertainment.

Jack gave Marie a discreet sign she seemed to understand perfectly.

'Let's get out of the way,' he said to Frances as he led her again towards the dressing room.

The last thing she heard was Marie tell Andie Miller loud enough for Mr Dunne to hear, 'I just heard the poor vet they've stitched up for that horrible murder didn't do it after all. I bet there'll be another arrest tomorrow.'

They left the dressing room door ajar as Frances and Jack listened for steps towards the office. *Please, let us be right*, she prayed silently.

Shuffling noises alerted them.

Jack inched the door open. They saw a man slipping into the office.

Frances wished she'd had time to take off the roller skates. Every tiny noise seemed magnified.

Jack touched a finger to his lips. She nodded.

They crept into the office. Mr Dunne squatted on his haunches as he rummaged in the open safe. A desk lamp shone directly into the opening.

Jack blew a whistle.

Mr Dunne spun around, a pistol in his hand. It gleamed menacingly in the low light. He rose to his full height.

'Your girl-friend will join me,' he said in a conversational tone that made Frances sick. 'Unless you want to find out what an excellent shot I am.'

Frances moved closer to Mr Dunne, hoping she'd cover Jack with her body.

Mr Dunne grabbed her with his free arm.

'I guess you're just as good with a syringe, and a horseshoe,' Jack said.

'Clever. Very clever.'

'You won't get away with it,' Jack said.

Mr Dunne waved the pistol from Frances to Jack. 'I think I already have. And if you two lovebirds have had a little bit too much to drink and crash my car, I'll be sure to send a wreath.'

Jack applauded.

'Stop that,' Mr Dunne said. 'No unnecessary noise, or your sweetheart here will feel first-hand what I'm capable of.'

Frances swayed. She told herself it was only to convince him that he'd won, and that it had nothing to do with fear. She was sure Jack had tried to cover up any sounds from the passage.

'If you hurt her ...' Jack clenched his fist.

'You're not exactly in a position to threaten me.'

'I know. If this were an act on the stage -' Jack lowered his gaze and looked despondent on the floor. And at her roller skates.

She drummed a beat on her thigh. One, two, three. Frances let herself loose control of the skates and crash heavily against Mr Dunne who lost his balance. Jack grabbed Mr Dunne's pistol hand and twisted it.

The pistol fell onto the floor. Frances scrambled to pick it up.

'I think we'll take over from here.' Phil entered together with Sergeant Miller. The sergeant pulled Mr Dunne to his feet and cuffed his hands behind his back.

'About bloody time,' Jack said.

'I didn't want to make his trigger finger itch,' Phil said with an apologetic glance at Frances. 'And you were so good at making him sing.'

Jack clapped Sergeant Miller on his shoulder. 'Thanks for pitching in on this job.'

'My pleasure,' the policeman said.

Phil picked up the telephone. 'You go back to your wife, Sergeant, and I wait here for reinforcements.'

'I'll wait with you,' Jack said. 'Frances, you go and have fun with Uncle Sal.'

'Are you sure?'

Phil turned around discreetly as Frances leant in and kissed Jack until they both had to come up for air.

'Absolutely,' he said. 'We can continue this conversation later.'

# CHAPTER TWENTY-NINE

*C*ockatoos screeched in the early morning sun. Rob stumbled through the prison gates like a somnambulist afraid of waking up.

'Rob.' Frances flung herself into her brother's arms. Tears rolled down her cheeks. He held onto her like a drowning man.

'I'm really not dreaming,' he said. She shook her head. His body felt so skinny to her touch, with his shoulder blades jutting out.

Jack leant against the bonnet of the Ford. They'd been waiting outside the prison since seven o'clock. If he and Uncle Sal had let her have her will, she'd camped here all night, fearful of having Rob find himself all alone.

Her brother climbed into the car, his dazed look unchanged. 'Where are we going?'

'Home,' she said. 'You're safe.'

Uncle Sal hugged Rob so hard, Frances thought she heard ribs crack. 'You sit down, my boy, and have a proper meal.'

～

Jack left them to their reunion, so Frances and Uncle Sal could give Rob their undivided attention.

He shovelled in eggs and bacon as if he'd been starving. Only when he'd wiped his greasy plate clean with a slice of fried bread did his face lose that haunted look.

'I am home alright. But I still haven't the foggiest why the charges were dropped.' He reached for their hands. 'What I am sure of is that it was you who got me off. You, and White Jack.'

'It was Mr Dunne all along,' Frances said. 'He'd been running a string of painted horses together with a few people in different cities. They'd use a couple of runners to place bets with bookies, blokes desperate for a bob or two and not likely to ask questions. The police have his ledger, with all the names and dates.'

'And Brocky? Poor devil, getting murdered for recognising a horse.'

'They found the poison used to kill him in Mr Dunne's safe,' Uncle Sal said.

'Did anyone else in Morphettville work with him?' Rob's hand trembled. 'I can't believe it. They all seemed like good fellows, you know.'

'No-one who had any clue what he was really up to, as far as we've been told,' Uncle Sal said. 'He might have gotten the idea from his dad, who used to work for the old lady in Hobart he used as a front. We'd have twigged it was him a lot sooner if we'd known the old man's real name, instead of only hearing about Old Pom with the sticky fingers.'

'And the other vet? Did he leave me in the soup?' Rob asked.

Frances hugged him again. 'He probably had an idea Mr Dunne was up to no good,' she said. 'Marie saw a brochure in his new surgery, about Charleston. We didn't understand until her friend Andie, who grew up there, mentioned the place was founded by a Mr Dunn. Maybe it was supposed to be some kind of security. Like, I've left a few clues if something happens to me.'

Rob's lids drooped.

'Bath and then bed,' Frances said. 'Tonight, we'll celebrate. But first you ring up Lucy and Mum.'

Frances had difficulties tearing her gaze away from Rob who sat in an upstairs niche at the Top Note with Tony and Pauline.

'It's fine if you want to join them.' Jack smiled into her upturned face. 'We can always dance another night.'

'No, he rarely has the chance to talk with Tony. What I'd love though is to repeat a bit of the show for Rob.'

Her brother was dead set on leaving Adelaide as soon as he could, to return to his wife and son. Phil had arranged for his statements to be taken as soon as possible and then it would be good-bye. He might not even have to stand witness against Mike Dunne, thanks to the overwhelming evidence.

'Sounds good to me.' Jack held her so close her heart fluttered. 'Tomorrow night? Dolores is dying to try out her swing seat here, without an investigation to distract us.'

He nodded towards the singer who floated by in Phil's arms. Her boyfriend had done his best to smooth everything for them, including glossing over the little details like picked locks and borrowed documents. He'd been fair enough to emphasise Sergeant Miller's part in the arrest, too. With any luck, the officer would receive a promotion, or at least a recommendation.

Rob's jaw dropped as he watched first Dolores and then his little sister on stage. Frances looked like she belonged there and not in a stuffy telephone exchange.

Jack sat next to him. 'Impressed?'

'I've seen Uncle Sal in action when I was a youngster, but my sister – wow.' Rob shook his head in admiration.

'Don't worry. I'll look after her.'

'I don't know how to thank you.' Rob swallowed. 'For everything.'

'No need. Anyone would have done the same.'

'I don't think so, but I'm grateful. Also, for your telling them not to ask too many questions.'

'I've never been in prison,' Jack said. 'But I have some experience with bad stuff you can't talk about, at least not straight away.'

'Yeah. It's like a bad dream at the moment.'

'If you do want to talk and don't want to burden your wife, we're here.'

Jack gave Rob's shoulder a light squeeze.

Bluey came sprinting up the stairs, a telegram in his hand.

'What on earth?' Jack asked as he took the telegram and slit it open.

He was still holding on to it as Uncle Sal, Frances and Pauline joined them.

'You're quiet,' Frances said.

'Just a bit tired,' he said. 'I'm not twenty anymore.'

She laughed. 'As if anyone could keep up with you.'

He pressed a kiss on her head. 'I'll leave you to enjoy yourselves. Bluey will drive you home whenever you're ready.'

# CHAPTER THIRTY

*J*ack dropped in while they were still at breakfast. Frances had to return to work the next day, and she wanted to make the most of these last precious hours.

Rob wanted to excuse himself as Jack entered the kitchen.

Jack waved it off. 'Please stay. There's a few things I'd like to talk with you all about.'

Frances dropped her toast. 'Is anything wrong?'

'Probably not. My mother has asked me to visit.'

'In England?' Frances voice shook. Having Jack travel to New Zealand had been bad enough. England was on the other side of the world!

'In England, or France. I couldn't quite make head or tail of it. The thing is, I'd like you to come along.'

'Me?' Frances couldn't believe her ears.

Jack addressed Rob. 'If I'm right, your mother would love to help your wife now that another baby's coming. I assume your Lucy is fine with that?'

'Too right she is. But we know that Mum has her home here, with Franny and Uncle Sal.'

Uncle Sal's jaw muscle twitched. 'If you can go, love, do it. You always wanted to travel.'

'I thought you'd come along as well,' Jack said. 'When I checked in with the travel agent, he asked me if you'd be willing to entertain the passengers on the ship. You and Signorina Francesca. He'd read an article in *"The Advertiser"*.'

'They want us?'

'Well, ideally they'd love to hire Dolores too, but she doesn't cope well with sea voyages. She got sick on the ferry to Kangaroo Island.'

Frances's head whirled. 'And the Top Note? And my job? What are Uncle Sal and I going to do in Europe?'

'You'll find something to occupy you. I thought Marie and Bluey could manage the club between them. I'm sure your boss will give you leave, if you tell him it's a family emergency, and it's going to be your honeymoon.'

Frances felt her jaw drop.

'My -'

'Unless you'd rather wait with our wedding until all our family can be assembled in one place. I might be old and grey before that happens.'

Frances stared at Jack until Rob nudged her. 'Say something.'

'You're not joking.'

'Never. We've got our fair share of entertainers already.'

'Yes,' she said. 'Please, Jack.'

He pulled her close.

Uncle Sal cleared his throat and motioned Rob to follow him.

Frances barely registered them leaving.

'You're crying.' Jack wiped a tear off her cheek.

'It's all been a bit much.'

'It's all over,' he said. 'From now on it'll all be smooth sailing. I promise.'

'A little adventure is alright though.'

'I'm glad to say that. Crossing the oceans end of the year can have its exciting moments.'

She snuggled into his arms.

'I'll have you and Uncle Sal to look after me.'

'You won't get rid of us.'

Another, slightly daunting, thought hit her. 'What if your mother won't like me?'

'She will.'

'Are you sure?'

'As sure as I've ever been. Now, who do want to talk to first, your mother or your boss? And how long does it take you to pack? We can buy everything you still need once we've docked in England.'

Her heart sang. 'We're really going?'

'I've already booked our cabins,' he said.

'What if I had said no?' She giggled.

'In that case I'm convinced Pauline would have been only too happy to have another shot at stardom. Although I would decline to marry her. I'll leave that to Tony.'

He stroked her cheek. 'I think we should let Rob and Uncle Sal back in. It gets a bit uncomfortable, eavesdropping on a door.'

Frances whispered into his ear. 'I love you.'

He smiled at her, with that special smile he only reserved for her. 'I'd drink to that, but not with coffee, or a Frances Palmer special.' Jack raised his voice. 'You can come in now.'

Rob had a sheepish look on his face as Jack shook his hand. 'Mum won't be happy if you have a wedding without her, but I'm glad for you.'

Uncle Sal kissed Jack on both cheeks, properly and not staged air-kisses. 'You're getting one in a million, son. Just so you know.'

'I do. I had that feeling right from the start.' He pulled Frances to him. 'The ship's leaving in six days. You'd better get a wiggle on.'

'Six days?' She snapped her mouth shut.

'Rob, I need you to help me in the attic.' Uncle Sal rubbed his hands. 'I have my knives, but there should be a few things we can use for magic tricks.'

They walked past Jack, in a happy discussion.

'I'll see you tonight,' Jack said. 'And one thing.'

'Yes?'

'I'm okay with whatever Uncle Sal cooks up, but if he turns you into a vanishing act, I'll put my foot down.'

'I'm not going to disappear. Ever.'

'Good. Because I won't let that happen, Mrs Jack.'

The End

ALSO BY CARMEN RADTKE

*False Play at the Christmas Party*

1928; a charity event in aid of veterans sounded like rich pickings ....

*A Matter of Love and Death*

An overheard conspiracy and a budding romance turn telephone operator Frances's life into a matter of love and death.

*The Case of the Missing Bride*

1862. A group of young Australian women set sail for matrimony in Canada, but somebody has different plans for them.

*Glittering Death*

Gold rush, wedding bells and murder. The Australian brides have arrived in Canada, but a murder shatters their new happiness.

*Walking in the Shadow*

New Zealand, 1909. Jimmy is the miracle man. But although

he is cured from an almost incurable disease, he gives up his newfound freedom to return to the small leprosy camp on Quail Island and cuts himself off from the world.